JESSI'S HORRIBLE PRANK

Every day the pranks in my Short Takes class were getting worse. The day before, Wednesday, half the class had turned its back on Mr Trout at John Rosen's signal. Thursday was Mr Trout's ninth day as our teacher. At this rate they'd be tarring and feathering him by next week.

The worst part was watching Mr Trout react. Sometimes he'd give a small, phony laugh. Other times he'd sigh and look slightly annoyed. But most of the time he did absolutely nothing.

JESSI'S HORRIBLE PRANK

Ann M. Martin

*The author gratefully acknowledges
Peter Lerangis for
his help in preparing this manuscript.*

Scholastic Children's Books,
Commonwealth House, 1-19 New Oxford Street,
London WC1A 1NU, UK
a division of Scholastic Ltd
London ~ New York ~ Toronto ~ Sydney ~ Auckland

First published in the US by Scholastic Inc., 1994
First published in the UK by Scholastic Ltd, 1996

Text copyright © Ann M. Martin, 1994
THE BABYSITTERS CLUB is a registered trademark of Scholastic Inc.

ISBN 0 590 13736 0

Typeset in Plantin by Contour Typesetters, Southall, London
Printed by Cox & Wyman Ltd, Reading, Berks.

10 9 8 7 6 5 4 3 2 1

1st CHAPTER

"What *are* you doing?"

Uh-oh! I had thought I was alone in the corridor. Instead I was caught red-handed by a classmate of mine, Sanjita Batts. Actually, red-*toed* was more like it. I confess, I was walking to my Short Takes class *en pointe*.

That is ballet terminology for "on the tips of your toes". And I mean the very tips. It's hard to do, especially for a sixth-grader like me.

Walking *en pointe* looks beautiful on stage. But in the corridor of Stoneybrook Middle School, it looks . . . well, daft.

So why was I doing it? Because I, Jessica Ramsey, am a dance fanatic. I *love* ballet and I want to be a professional dancer one day. Even if it means having mangled toes the rest of my life. (Have you ever *seen* a

1

ballerina's feet? They're frightening.)

"Just practising," I said, lowering myself to a normal walking position.

"Don't stop." Sanji had a mischievous glint in her eye. "You should walk into class like that!"

"No way!" I replied.

"Seriously! Can you imagine the look on Mr Trout's face?"

I couldn't help giggling. We get a new Short Takes teacher every term, and our latest one, Mr Trout, was a bit of a nerd.

Every student at Stoneybrook Middle School has Short Takes for one period a day. It's a special programme of revolving courses. No, the room doesn't turn in a slow circle like one of those posh hotel restaurants. What I mean is, every six weeks we get a new subject and a new teacher. What kind of subjects? Unusual ones, like Stress Reduction for Teenagers; or Project Work, in which we all have to do after-school jobs in the community (I worked in a cinema).

Our current class was called Software from Scratch, which was really another way of saying Computer Programming.

Computer programs are a bit like dances. On the outside they both look fun and easy. But behind every graceful ballet is a lot of sweating and grunting and muscle strain and step-by-step memorizing. And behind every cool graphics program are a million or so lines of gobbledygook.

That's what our Short Takes class was about. Creating the gobbledygook.

Yawn. Give me an hour a day of dance warm-ups *any* time.

As Sanjita and I made our way to the class, we heard the loud clattering of high heels from around the corner ahead of us.

"Quick," Sanji whispered. "Dolly One or Two?"

"Er . . . Two," I said.

I was wrong. Miss Bernhardt, otherwise known as Dolly One, bounced around the corner towards us. Her thick blonde hair looked as if it were trampolining on her head.

Dolly Two is another teacher, Miss Vandela. The two Dollies, as you can guess, look alike. They're short and big-busted. They both have huge smiles and Major Hair that cascades in ringlets over their shoulders. They also wear tons of make-up. You've probably already worked out how they got their nicknames. Right. They're both Dolly Parton clones—and Dolly Parton *fans*, so they don't mind their nicknames at all. (In case you don't know, Dolly Parton is a famous country and western singer who fits the above description.)

"Hi, girls!" Dolly One chirped as she bustled past with a clipboard. "I'm putting up signing-up sheets for the Follies."

"Already?" Sanji asked.

"It's springtime, darling," Dolly One replied. "Now, I want both of you to think about signing up. We want to get a good cross-section of the school!"

"OK," Sanji said.

I should explain something. Sanjita is Puerto Rican and I'm African-American. Stoneybrook is a mostly white town. What Dolly One meant by *cross*-section was "not only white students".

Now, I knew she was only trying to be fair. She's a nice person, and she wanted to make sure Sanji and I didn't feel excluded. But statements like that make me feel funny. They remind me how different I am in some people's eyes.

I didn't always feel so different. In Oakley, New Jersey, where I grew up, people of all colours lived together and no one made a big deal about it. But when my family moved to Stoneybrook before sixth grade started, we were in for a shock. Some people were really cold to us, as if we didn't belong. Others seemed afraid to be near us. Kids were hostile to me at school. It was *awful* for a while. Luckily, things have improved a lot since then. Stoneybrook has turned out to be a great place, and I made the best friends in the world when I joined the Babysitters Club (which I'll tell you about later).

Anyway, I was dying to find out about the show. As Miss Bernhardt clickety-clacked down the hallway, I asked Sanjita, "What are the Follies?"

"You know, the Sixth-Grade Follies," Sanji said. "Where the sixth-graders make up songs and sketches and things. SMS has one every year."

I shrugged. "I didn't live here last year."

"Well, it's hilarious. My big sister was in last year's. The students write the whole show. You get to do imitations and make fun of teachers, students, the school—everything." Then she laughed and added, "Probably even walk on your toes, if you want."

"Are you going to sign up?" I asked.

"No way. I get stage fright. You?"

"I might."

Might? Gosh! An end-of-the-year show, all original stuff—it sounded perfect. I *love* making people laugh. I was the comedy highlight of a school production of *Peter Pan* (well, I was). And with my dance

5

experience, maybe I'd be able to choreograph and perform.

I was flying high as we walked into our Short Takes class.

Mr Trout was scribbling something on the blackboard. His eyes darted towards Sanji and me.

"Hello, Mr Trout," Sanji said in a voice that was so friendly it sounded phony.

He looked back at the board, adjusted his glasses, and grunted a soft "Hi."

Sanji glanced at me, rolled her eyes, and giggled. We both sat down as the bell rang.

To my right, John Rosen and Mark O'Connell were playing noughts and crosses, passing a sheet of paper to and fro. To my left, Sandra Hart was reading a comic book. A spitball flew across the room and landed in Renee Johnson's hair. Two boys burst out laughing.

"*Ugh!*" Renee shouted. "That's disgusting! Mr Trout, Craig and George are throwing spitballs."

Mr Trout turned around. Instead of looking angry or annoyed, he looked . . . lost. If you didn't know he was a teacher, you'd think he was worried that Craig and George would reprimand *him*. "Er, that's enough, now," he said, twirling the chalk in his fingers. "OK?"

The two boys just giggled again. The rest

of my classmates could hardly hold in their laughter. Sanjita's hand was over her mouth and she was turning purple.

I admit, I had the urge to laugh, too. You have to picture Mr Trout. He's about six feet tall and extremely skinny, with this waxy black hair combed in a style right out of the 1970s. His trousers are too big and always bag over his shoes. He alternates between two tweed jackets from day to day, which he wears over old check shirts with plastic pocket protectors.

What's worse, sometimes he pronounces his *r*'s a little like *w*'s. Just slightly, though, and only when he's *extremely* nervous.

"All right, can anyone come to the board and write the last lines of this program?" Mr Trout asked.

From the back of the class, I could hear Maria Fazio whisper, "Wite the wast wines of this pwogwam?"

A few kids around her cracked up. John and Mark sniggered and kept playing noughts and crosses. Sandra buried her face in her comic book. Sanjita let out a big yawn. No one volunteered.

I couldn't believe how rude they all were. Any other teacher would have yelled, or made a joke like "Don't all speak at once," or called on someone to answer the question.

Not Mr Trout. He just fidgeted and looked helpless.

My good mood was taking a nosedive. His nervousness was making *me* nervous. I wanted to put up my hand, but I would have looked so dorky.

As the class began settling down, Sanjita passed me a note that looked like this:

I tried to stifle a laugh. It came out sounding like a pig snort. Very elegant.

Well, needless to say, the class went by slowly. Luckily, though, everyone settled down. And I managed to stay awake right till the end.

Short Takes is my third class of the day. Five classes later, school was over. But before leaving, I had to make two stops. The first was the main corridor, where I signed my name on the Follies sheet. (At the bottom was an announcement that the first planning meeting would be on Thursday, only three days away.)

As I was writing, I heard a familiar voice say, "Ooh, you're going to be in the show! Great! You'll be *so* funny!"

"Hi, Mal!" I replied.

Mallory Pike is my very best friend ever. We can talk about *anything*. (She laughs at all my jokes too.) She's the only person I know who's as crazy about horse stories as I am. Marguerite Henry books, *The Black Stallion* series, *The Saddle Club*—we've read them all. One day we'll be talking about Mal's books! She's an incredibly talented writer and illustrator.

"Are you going to sign up?" I asked.

"I'll just watch," she said.

Mal doesn't like performing. During a school production of *Peter Pan*, she was in charge of costumes. She's also just got over a bout of glandular fever, so I think she wanted to take it easy.

Together we walked to my second stop, the front steps of the school. That's where our BSC friends always meet to chat at the end of the day.

We walked into a very serious conversation between Claudia Kishi and Kristy Thomas.

"I'd never do it," Kristy was saying, arms folded. "Not in a million years."

"I would," Claudia replied. "I mean, I *might*. Just for fun."

"Fun? It would be *permanent*, Claud. No going back. What happens years from now, when you have to look for a job?"

Claudia laughed. "You don't wear it. Who's going to know?"

"What if they just happen to look up your nostrils?" Kristy asked.

"Gross, Kristy!"

I couldn't help barging in. "What are you lot *talking* about?"

"Nose rings," Kristy replied. "Can you believe it? Claud wants to have her nose pierced."

"Kristy, I didn't say I *wanted* to," Claudia insisted. "All I said was nose jewellery looks cool."

"Oh, yeah, great," Kristy replied, "if you want to look like Daisy the Cow."

Claudia rolled her eyes. "You get the *side* of your nose pierced, not the middle."

"Who looks like Daisy the Cow?"

We all turned at the sound of Mary Anne Spier's voice. She was walking towards us with Stacey McGill. "No one," I said. "Yet."

10

"Mooooo!" moaned Claudia. She had taken off one of her clip-on earrings and somehow clasped it on to her nose.

We all burst out laughing. Claudia quickly took the earring off and wrinkled up her nose.

"Ow! That hurt. I've changed my mind."

"Good," Kristy said. She looked at her watch, then at the line of buses. "Oops! See you lot later!"

"'Bye!" we called out as she sprinted for her bus.

Stoneybrook is part suburban, part rural and part posh. Most of us live in the suburban part, within walking distance of school, but Kristy lives in a mansion, right on the other side of town in the posh part. However, Kristy is about as non-posh as can be. (Her stepfather's a millionaire, which is a long story I'll leave for later.)

The rest of us began walking home, discussing nose jewellery. I think it's great, but let's face it, it takes a while for some African styles to catch on. Claudia was really the only other one who liked the idea. Stacey admitted it looked OK, but only on other people.

When I got home, my aunt Cecelia was waiting outside the house, looking very cross. (She's my dad's sister, and she lives with us.) My sister Becca, who's eight, was running round from behind the house.

"I can't find him, Aunt Cecelia," Becca said.

"Oh my lord, that boy will be the death of me!" Aunt Cecelia replied. "*John Philip! Where are you?*"

"Squirt!" Becca called out.

John Philip and Squirt are the same person, my baby brother. He popped out from behind a bush, yelling, "Worrr!"

"Aah! A dinosaur!" Becca squealed.

Squirt shrieked with excitement. Then he raised his hands over his head and repeated, "Worrr!" (That's his way of roaring.)

My brother is a toddler. He's the sweetest child alive. Aunt Cecelia is about fifty or so. Sweet isn't the word I'd use to describe her. *Severe*, maybe. She moved in with us to look after Squirt when my mum went back to work. It was hard to get used to her. She's relaxed since then, but she can still be a pain sometimes. The strange thing is, my dad's about the most easy-going man in the world. Oh, well, I suppose Aunt Cecelia has got enough sourness for two people.

She was scowling at Squirt, hands on hips. "Young man, I do not want to see you hiding behind those bushes again."

"He can't understand you, Aunt Cecelia," I volunteered.

"Dess-seee!" Squirt shrieked, toddling

towards me with wide open arms.

"Hi, Squirt! Hi, everyone!" I called out.

"Oh, he most certainly can!" Aunt Cecelia replied. "They understand much more than you think!" Then, as an afterthought, she added, "Hello, Jessica."

I scooped up Squirt and nuzzled his tummy. He giggled uncontrollably and then said, "Ah-*den*!" (That's *again* in his private language, which we call Squirt-glish.)

"Sandwich!" Becca yelled. She wrapped her arms around me, trapping our brother between us. "We're the bread and Squirt is the peanut butter!" That made Squirt wriggle *and* giggle. Aunt Cecelia shook her head and said, "You girls spoil him."

But I could see the sides of her mouth curling up into a smile.

Squirt squirmed out from between the pieces of bread and screamed, "Duck, duck, doose!"

Well, we played that about a hundred times. Then we played hide-and-seek, but Squirt kept hiding in the same two places. Afterwards he wanted to be lifted up like a "heckopper" (helicopter). That's when Aunt Cecelia gave up.

By five o'clock we were still playing. Well, Squirt was. I was exhausted.

Honk! Honk!

Daddy's car pulled into the drive. He had

picked up Mama, and they were both giving us huge smiles from the front seat.

"Day-eee! Mummumm!" Squirt began running towards the car.

"Careful!" Aunt Cecelia called out from the front porch.

Squirt fell forward on the lawn. He immediately sat up and stared at his hands, which were covered with freshly cut grass.

"Blind-side tackle!" Daddy bellowed as he got out of the car. He fell to the ground and wrestled with Squirt, who screamed with joy.

Becca and I joined the pile-up. Mama leaned over us and managed to kiss us all.

"John! Your shirt!" Aunt Cecelia warned.

Daddy sat up. Grass clung to his white shirt, along with thin green stains.

He pretended to be shocked and looked around at all of us. "Who did this to me? Do you realize how much work Aunt Cecelia is going to have to do? Arrrrgh!"

He sprang to his feet and began chasing us round the garden.

Among our shrieks and giggles, I could hear Aunt Cecelia's voice saying, "How much work *who's* going to do?"

I thought Mama was going to die laughing.

Welcome to the Ramsey family.

2nd CHAPTER

"Remember Mr Steinmetz?" Claudia asked.

Kristy and Mary Anne howled. "He was a caretaker," Mary Anne explained, "who had a missing front tooth."

"Every time he said an *S*, he whistled," Kristy went on. "Like, Misshhhhter Shhh-teinmetshhh—oh, I can't do it."

"But Alan Gray could!" Claudia chimed in.

Kristy mumbled, "That's the only thing he's good for." (Alan Gray is Eighth-Grade Enemy Number One.)

"Well, he did the funniest imitation," Mary Anne said. "I thought I'd never stop laughing—but I felt so *awful*!"

"Oh, Mr Steinmetz didn't mind," Kristy reminded her. "He laughed so hard he almost keeled over on the floor."

15

It was 5:28 that Monday afternoon, the day I'd signed up for the Follies. Our Babysitters Club meeting was about to begin, and guess what we were talking about?

The Follies of two years ago. I had walked into Claudia's bedroom (the BSC headquarters) talking about our Follies with Mallory. That was when Kristy, Claudia and Mary Anne started telling us *their* experiences.

Those three, by the way, are part of The Big Four, the first BSC members. (The Fourth is Stacey.)

Actually the club began with the Big *One*, Kristy.

OK, I said I'd tell you all about the BSC so here goes:

A History of the Babysitters Club
by Jessica Ramsey

It was a dark and stormy night in Stoneybrook, Connecticut. Time and time again, a telephone receiver slammed in the Thomas house. "Woe is me," cried Mrs Thomas, "for I cannot find a suitable person to watch over my youngest offspring, and my three eldest are unavailable tonight."

Alas, my heart aches to see my mother in such distress, thought Kristy. *Alone with four children, abandoned by a husband (my father), and deserving of a night out. Oh, if*

16

only there were a single phone number at which she might reach a group of reliable sitters.

Kristy stood up, struck by inspiration. Quickly she called her two best friends, Claudia Kishi and Mary Anne Spier.

"Hark! Hear my plan," announced Kristy to each. "Let us meet regularly—Monday, Wednesday and Friday, between 5:30 and 6:00. Let us elect officers, and have a telephone! Henceforth, at those appointed times, the parents in our fair village may secure the services of whoever shall join me in this historic enterprise."

"I shall ask my friend Stacey to join," said Claudia.

With exclamations of joy and triumph, the Babysitters Club was born. Quickly its fame grew, and the club expanded to nine members. Stoneybrook lived happily ever after, as did Mrs Thomas, who married a millionaire.

The End

Well, *something* like that.

In plain English, the BSC meets to answer phone calls from parents who need babysitters. With so many members, we can cover almost all job requests. Parents are happy because they know they'll get a good sitter with just one call. *We're* happy because we get lots of jobs.

All from the amazing mind of Kristy.

And I do mean amazing. You could put her in the desert and she'd work out how to make it rain. She's constantly dreaming up ways to solve problems. She didn't just invent the BSC; she set up all the rules and traditions, including (1) a record book that contains a job calendar, a list of clients (complete with addresses, phone numbers and rates paid), and a description of our charges' likes and dislikes; (2) a notebook in which we write about our job experiences; and (3) Kid-Kits, which are small toy-and-game-filled boxes we sometimes take with us on sitting jobs.

What's Kristy like? Short and noisy (well, she *is*). But also friendly and down-to-earth, even though, as I mentioned, she lives in the posh part of Stoneybrook. She's got plain brown hair, and she *lives* in jeans and sweatshirts. She's also a terrific athlete. And she doesn't just play sport, she coaches, too—a team called Kristy's Krushers, which she organized herself. It's made up of kids too young or too clumsy or too shy for Little League. They play another team, Bart's Bashers, which is coached by Bart Taylor.

Bart and Kristy are an item. (I can't say any more. Kristy would kill me.)

You wouldn't believe the size of Kristy's house. It never feels crowded, even though

18

ten people live in it. Yes, *ten*. Watson Brewer, Kristy's stepfather, has two kids from a previous marriage (Karen and Andrew), who live there every other month. When Kristy, her mum, and her three brothers (seventeen-year-old Charlie, fifteen-year-old Sam, and seven-year-old David Michael) moved in, that made eight. Then Kristy's parents adopted a little girl called Emily Michelle (who's two) and Kristy's grandmother (Nannie) moved in. (Ten.)

Click

Claudia's digital clock flipped to 5:30. In the middle of a sentence, Kristy interrupted herself to say, "This meeting will come to order!"

Did you work out that Kristy's the BSC chairman? She is. And she hardly ever misses the click of 5:30. I bet, for the rest of her life, she'll say "Order!" at 5:30 on Mondays, Wednesdays and Fridays.

"Any new business?" Kristy asked.

Claudia, who had been handing around a huge bag of tortilla crisps, thrust it at Kristy. "Try these."

Kristy grabbed a fistful of crisps and shoved some in her mouth. "Pooey goo," she mumbled.

"Say it, don't spray it," Stacey McGill

19

said, pretending (I think) to wipe off some damp crisp crumbs.

Kristy swallowed. "Pretty good."

"They're baked, not fried," Claudia remarked. "Which means you can eat, like, three times as many."

Grinning, she reached under her bed and pulled out two more bags.

Claud's room is the official BSC headquarters (because she's got her own phone), but a better name for it might be *hide*-quarters. You can't pick up a thing in there without discovering sweets, biscuits, crisps, pretzels or Nancy Drew books. She hides them because her parents allow only Wholesome Foods and Great Literature in the house. (Silly isn't it? As Claudia says, "There's more to life than *Johnny Tremain* and brussels sprouts.")

Claudia once thought she was adopted (untrue), because she's so different from the rest of her strait-laced family. They're all clever (her older sister, Janine, is a certified genius), and none of them is interested in art. Claud's a pretty rotten student but a fabulous artist—in watercolour, sculpture, drawing, *everything*. (Maybe she gets her artistic inspiration from eating all that junk food.)

Can you picture Claudia? Fat? Nope. She looks like a model, slim and blemish-free. (I don't know how she does it.) She's got the most gorgeous Japanese features, silky black hair and almond-shaped eyes. Also, she always puts together the coolest outfits, mostly from stuff she finds in street markets. For example, at that meeting she was wearing '50s-style cat's-eye glasses frames, a plastic hairslide in the shape of an alligator, a tie-dyed T-shirt and bell-bottoms. And it looked fantastic.

Officially, Claudia's the BSC vice-chairman, although she could be called Chief Sugar Supplier or something.

Not for everybody, though. One of our members, Stacey, can't eat sweets. She's a diabetic, which means her body is unable to regulate the amount of sugar in her blood-stream. So she has to give herself (warning: if you've got a weak stomach, skip to the next paragraph) daily injections of something called insulin.

Which is why Claudia also stocks up on pretzels, crisps and other sugar-free goodies.

Stacey is one of the BSC's three blondes. She's also our *only* maths whiz, so she gets to be treasurer. Lucky her. She listens to us moan and groan as we give her our subs every Monday. Then she divides up the money for our expenses—helping Claudia pay her phone bill, restocking our Kid-Kits, and so on.

Like Claud, Stacey's a stunning dresser. Unlike Claud, she wouldn't be caught dead in a street market. She likes up-to-the-minute fashions. "Urban chic," she once described her style (sounds snobby, I know—but she's not). She grew up in New York City, the fashion capital of the world—and the dance capital, if you ask me. And theatre, and restaurant, and museum . . . do I sound jealous? I am. I ♥ the Big Apple!

How did Stacey end up in Stoneybrook? Well, first her dad's job brought her family here. Then her dad's job took them back to NYC. Then her parents got divorced, and Stacey moved back here with her mum.

Confusing? Well, it isn't ideal, but it has its good points: Stacey gets to live here and visit her dad in New York. (And sometimes we get to go with her.)

Mary Anne Spier is our other Big Apple freak. She's the only non-New Yorker I know who has mastered the subway system.

That's not surprising, because Mary Anne is the world's most organized person. As BSC secretary, she has to be. Her job is to handle the record book. The moment a request comes in, Mary Anne has to know (1) who's available, (2) who isn't free (because of doctors appointments, ballet classes and so on) and (3) how to share out jobs fairly, so everyone gets a roughly equal number. Then she records the job on the official calendar. (And she has never, *ever* made a mistake.)

Mary Anne is Kristy's best friend. They actually look rather alike—petite, with brown hair and dark eyes—but their personalities couldn't be more different. Mary Anne is shy and sensitive, and she hates sport. She cries at the slightest thing. She's read *Wuthering Heights* three times, and the pages of her book are wrinkled from teardrops.

Mary Anne's life is rather like a sad novel with a happy ending. Her mum died when she was a baby. Mr Spier was too distraught to look after Mary Anne, so he sent her away to her grandparents—and then he had to fight to get her back. To prove he could be a good single parent, he brought Mary Anne up very strictly. For years she had to go to bed early and dress in little-girl clothes. But one day, when Mary Anne was in seventh grade, a new girl moved to Stoneybrook and changed Mary Anne's life. Her name was Dawn Schafer and she came from California. Her parents had just got divorced, and her mum had decided to move back to her own home town, Stoneybrook. Well,

Dawn joined the Babysitters Club—and she and Mary Anne discovered that Mr Spier and Mrs Schafer had been high-school sweethearts! And guess who fell in love again?

Dum-dum-de-dum! (Wedding bells.)

After the wedding, Mary Anne and her dad moved into the Schafers' rambling old farmhouse. All of a sudden Mary Anne had a mum, a big new house, a happy and less strict dad, and a stepsister who was in the BSC. What a perfect ending . . . almost. The only trouble is, Dawn recently got incredibly homesick for California, so now she's back there for an extended visit.

We *all* miss her. Dawn's wonderful. She's really committed to some serious causes—the environment, health and fighting sexism. She eats only health foods: organic veggies and fruits, no red meat, no sweets. I admire her, even though I prefer a nice juicy hamburger to tofu any time.

Dawn (when she's here) is the BSC's alternate officer, which means she takes over when anyone's absent. She's blonde, but her hair is much lighter than Stacey's. Out in California, she belongs to a babysitting organization called the We ♥ Kids Club. (*All* the members are health-food eaters. They'd have heart attacks if Claudia moved to California.)

All the BSCers I've just mentioned are eighth-graders, two years older than Mallory and me. We young'uns are called junior members. We don't have official responsibilities, and because both our sets of parents think we're babies, we can't take late babysitting jobs. (Grrrr!) Actually, it's not too awful. The club gets plenty of requests for afternoon and weekend jobs.

Lots of those jobs are at Mal's house. Did I tell you Mal has *seven* younger siblings, including a set of triplets? It's true. Babysitting at her house is like going to a circus.

OK. Now you know that (a) the BSC is very busy, and (b) we've lost one member to California. You may be wondering how we cope with this problem. Leave it to Kristy. Soon after the club started, she decided we should have *associate* members. They fill in during emergencies but don't have to come to meetings or pay subs.

One of our associates, Shannon Kilbourne, has become Dawn's "pitch-hitter" (in the words of Coach Kristy). Shannon, who lives opposite Kristy, goes to a private school called Stoneybrook Day School. She's involved in lots of extra-curricular activities there, but somehow she manages to take on plenty of babysitting jobs, too.

Shannon's got really thick, curly, dark blonde hair and blue eyes.

Our other associate member is a boy. Well, not just any boy. He's Mary Anne's boyfriend, Logan Bruno. I suppose he's good-looking. Everybody says he is. He *is* a terrific sitter, but he tries to keep a low profile because his friends make fun of him. I hope they'll grow out of it one day, but you know boys!

Anyway, back to our meeting.

Rrriing!

"Hello, Babysitters Club!" Claudia said, picking up the receiver. "Hi, Dr Johanssen. Of course. I'll call you right back."

"Three weeks from Wednesday for Charlotte Johanssen?"

"*Three weeks?*" Shannon exclaimed.

"You know Charlotte's mum—*turbo-organized*," Stacey replied.

Mary Anne looked up from the record book. "Everyone's free. Want to do it, Stace?" (Stacey and Charlotte are very close.)

"Shhhhtashhhhey?" Kristy said, trying to whistle her *S*'s.

"OK, Mr Steinmetz," Stacey said, cracking up.

Claudia shook her head. "All those in favour of getting Alan Gray in here to give Kristy some lessons, say aye."

"*Aye!*" Mallory, Stacey, Mary Anne, Shannon and I yelled.

"Aargh!" Kristy screamed. "I'll never do it again! I promise!"

And she didn't.

But her imitation got me thinking again. Of the Follies.

Or I should say, The SMS Annual Sixth-Grade Follies, Starring Jessica Ramsey!

Well, I could dream, couldn't I?

3rd CHAPTER

EXACLY 10 MINS
BEFORE THE END OF CLASS,
WE WILL ALL DORP OUR
BOOKS ON THE FLOOR AT
THE SAME TIME.
PASS THIS NOTE ON !!!!!!!!!

Oh, groan!

I stared at the note Janet O'Neal had handed me. This was stupid. The oldest trick in the book.

Every day the pranks in my Short Takes class were getting worse. The day before, Wednesday, half the class had turned its back on Mr Trout at John Rosen's signal. Thursday was Mr Trout's ninth day as our teacher. At this rate they'd be tarring and feathering him by next week.

The worst part was watching Mr Trout react. Sometimes he'd give a small, phony laugh. Other times he'd sigh and look slightly annoyed. But most of the time he did absolutely nothing.

That just made everybody braver. Even Justine Moss, the shyest girl in the class, had joined in the back-turning prank.

It was awful. Dweeb or no dweeb, Mr Trout was a human being. He had to have feelings, even though he didn't show them. He was bound to break sooner or later. Part of me hoped he would get angry and keep the whole class for detention. That would stop the fooling around.

Mr Trout turned to the class, pointing to a short program he'd written. "Who wants to tell me how to de-bug this?"

"With de fly swatter?" Mark O'Connell called out.

Giggles all around.

"Come *on*, you lot!" protested Renee Johnson.

"Come on, you lot," Craig Avazian imitated, in a high-pitched voice.

"Mr Trout, he's making fun of me!" Renee said.

"Mr Trout, he's making fun of me!" Craig repeated.

Ugh!

This went on for a while, until Renee just stopped talking. By the time Mr Trout tried to draw our attention back to the blackboard, I'd forgotten what the program was about.

"*Pass it on, Jess!*" hissed Janet behind me.

Oops! I still had the note. I tapped the guy in front of me, Jimmy Bouloukos, on the shoulder and gave it to him. He laughed and immediately slipped it to the next person.

For the rest of the class, I couldn't concentrate. The examples on the board looked like hieroglyphics. All around me, kids were staring at the clock. Mr Trout gave up calling on volunteers and just lectured the whole time. My mind kept wandering to the Sixth-Grade Follies meeting, which was going to be held after school.

At fourteen minutes before the end of

class, Mr Trout was droning on about things called hexadecimals.

At thirteen minutes, he started writing on the blackboard.

At twelve, he was still writing. Kids were quietly piling up their books. Renee looked absolutely disgusted.

At eleven, even Renee was gathering her books.

That day, Sanjita was sitting right behind me. I could feel her staring at me quizzically. She tapped me on my back, as if to say, "Don't forget."

I was now the only person not getting ready. Twenty other kids surrounded me, fingers wrapped around neat piles of books. The clock's second hand was sweeping around, approaching the final time.

Imagine how I felt.

Not doing anything would be like betraying my classmates. If they were kept for detention, and *I* went free, I'd never hear the end of it.

But that was a big *if*. Chances were Mr Trout wouldn't do anything. Then I'd have to explain why I was too chicken to go along.

Calm down, Jessi, I told myself. It's just a joke.

The second hand was passing 9 on the clock. Fifteen seconds to go.

With a sigh, I quickly shuffled all my stuff together.

Five ... four ... three ... two ... one ... *WHAAAAAAMMM!*

The books hit the floor like a bomb.

Mr Trout squealed. That's the only way to describe the sound he made. He leaped off the ground, too, and his chalk flew out of his hand.

Then ... he screamed at the top of his lungs, made us pick up each book with our teeth, and took us all to the head teacher's office.

Wrong.

This is what he really did: First he adjusted his glasses. Then he cleared his throat. Finally he picked up the shattered pieces of chalk from the floor, took the largest chunk, and went right back to the program on the board.

No scolding, no detention, no nothing.

Maria started sniggering, then Craig and John. Before long Renee was laughing, too.

And so was I. I couldn't help it.

Not because it was so funny. It wasn't really. It was rather sad. I supposed I was laughing out of relief that Mr Trout hadn't blown up.

At the end of class, Mr Trout didn't even look up from his desk as we filed out.

A few kids gathered in the corridor to talk

about the prank. Not me. I wanted to get away from there as fast as possible.

The rest of the day flew by. At the sound of the end-of-school bell, I ran to the assembly hall.

The two Dollies were busily setting up a VCR and a TV on a trolley.

I was the first student there.

"Jessi, hi!" Miss Bernhardt (Dolly One) greeted me. "Do you know anything about plugging in VCRs?"

"I think I've worked it out," Miss Vandela (Dolly Two) announced.

I joined them behind the trolley. Miss Vandela was muttering. "Now, VCR In goes to TV Out, right?"

"Right!" Miss Bernhardt and I chimed in.

Miss Vandela held out a red wire. "So where does this go?"

Miss Bernhardt shrugged. "Just hold onto it, Dolly Sister. When we turn it on, see what happens to your perm."

The two of them cracked up.

I knew I was going to enjoy this. The Dollies were fun.

More students filed into the hall, and a couple of kids who were technically minded came to help us out. Then, when it was all set up, Miss Bernhardt quietened the group down and gave a little speech.

About twenty of us had gathered. We were all crowded together in seats near the TV.

"Welcome, everybody!" Miss Bernhardt said. "Now, Miss Vandela and I are new to the Follies this year, but we both have a little experience in theatre—and we're determined to make this year's show the best in history!"

We all cheered.

"And to start things off, we're going to show you a video with excerpts from last year's show. Roll 'em!"

Well, that video was one of the funniest things I'd ever seen. One group of kids did a sketch called "Gym for Teachers". Wearing potbellies, fake moustaches and clodhopper shoes, they imitated SMS teachers huffing and puffing in gym class.

Kate Condos led a number called "The SMS Rap", during which she pulled our head teacher, Mr Taylor, out from the audience, and made him dance along. Another kid did a comedy routine, and a group of four performed a great tap number.

I was really impressed.

By the end of the video, the whole group was bubbling with excitement.

Miss Vandela took over then. "We have some special plans," she announced. "For the first time, the Sixth-Grade Follies will be a benefit concert. We'll be charging admission, and donating the profits to a worthy organization. This means we'll need two important committees.

"The performance committee will be in charge of planning the show," Miss Vandela continued. "That means deciding on a title and theme, working out the format, writing the material, helping to audition performers, and setting up sub-committees—like make-up and lighting. I must stress, though, that we want *everyone* to audition, even committee members."

A couple of kids groaned.

"It's just so we can get an idea of everyone's talent, that's all," Miss Bernhardt said. "Very low pressure. Now, the *finance* committee will choose the charity we'll donate our proceeds to, as well as organize the collection of money. May I have volunteers for the performance committee?"

I put my hand up.

"Finance?"

I put it up again.

Miss Bernhardt wrote me down for both.

I couldn't wait to begin work.

4th CHAPTER

"After much consideration blah blah bell curve mumble mumble perhaps the difficulty level exceeded expectations blah blah."

That wasn't exactly what Mr Trout said. But it was something like that. I think he was trying to explain that we'd all failed our first test.

Yes, test.

It had been a complete surprise. Last Friday, he had passed out photocopied sheets of computer gobbledygook. "A simple BASIC program," he had called it. (Or was it a "basic SIMPLE program"?)

Well, it wasn't either—simple *or* basic. I didn't understand a thing. I thought he'd made a mistake and given us a test in Ancient Greek.

I was horrified. Afterwards, I talked to some classmates. It turned out *no one* had known how to answer the problems.

Now we were all facing the consequences.

Mr Trout fiddled with a propelling pencil, then tucked it behind his left ear. "As a result of the low scores, I have decided to cancel everyone's grades and devote a few days to rigorous revision."

Big mistake. I mean, it didn't sound like "wigowous wevision" to me, but it must have to Maria Fazio, because she was having a cow in the back of the class.

I turned and gave her a Look. So did Renee and a couple of others.

Luckily, several kids were cheering about the grade cancellation. Mr Trout didn't seem to hear Maria.

Actually, he seemed preoccupied with something on his desk. Or something *not* on his desk. He looked under his grade book, which had all our test papers tucked into it. Then he bent down and scanned the floor.

"That's odd . . ." he said under his breath. "I just had it in my hand. . ."

He reached into his trouser pocket, then into his shirt pocket protector (which was empty).

He turned to the right, scratching his head. His propelling pencil was facing us now, still nestled behind his ear.

Oops!

I began to put up my hand to tell him, but Janet reached from behind me and pulled it down.

When I turned to face her, she was smiling. She put her finger to her lips to shush me.

Around us, kids were catching on. Everyone was trying hard not to crack up.

I faced forward again. Mr Trout was sitting at his desk, rummaging through his drawer. A box of paper clips fell out on to the floor.

"Oh, dear. . ." he said.

He pushed the drawer closed and dropped to his knees.

Rrrrrrrip.

His tie had got caught in the drawer. It must have been old, because it tore right off at the collar.

"Oh!" Mr Trout exclaimed.

This was too much. No one could hold it in. The whole class was whooping. It sounded like canned laughter in a TV sitcom.

Mr Trout quickly took off what was left of his tie and began picking up the paper clips. I felt so sorry for him. But my stomach was in knots from laughing. If only he would say something—chuckle, *anything*—this whole thing wouldn't be so embarrassing. Or so funny.

While Mr Trout was kneeling, Jimmy Bouloukos sneaked up to the desk and swiped the grade book. He rushed back to his own desk and stuffed it inside.

When Mr Trout finally stood up, his pencil was back in his pocket protector. Beads of sweat had formed just beneath his strange, thick hair. He dumped the paper clips back in his desk and said, "Now we can settle down to. . ."

His voice drifted off. He was staring at the desk again. No one said a word about Jimmy.

He opened his desk drawer again, looked inside, and closed it.

"Hmmm . . . er. . ." You could tell he was about to ask about the book, but thought better of it. He probably thought he'd left it somewhere obvious and didn't want to humiliate himself again.

I wanted to laugh. My stomach was convulsing.

Turning to the blackboard, Mr Trout said, "Now then, let me write out the first problem. . ."

Someone piped up, "*Twout!*" in the back of the class, more like a strange animal noise than a word.

Mr Trout looked over his shoulder. "I

beg your pardon? Does someone have a question?"

"Just had something between my teeth," George Weiss said (whatever *that* meant).

If I were George's teacher, I would have said something. Mr Trout just nodded and turned back to the board.

Then someone else chimed in, "*Twout!*"

"You see," Mr Trout said, either ignoring or not hearing the sound effects, "at this step, we must ensure the programme does not result in an endless loop—"

"*Twout!*"

"*Twout!*"

Great. The class had turned into a pool of barking seals.

This kind of thing continued the rest of the hour. At one point, when Mr Trout was busy writing on the board, Jimmy put back the grade book.

If Mr Trout was surprised, he didn't show it. He just kept trying to teach, as if nothing was wrong.

He never did give back those test papers, which was probably just as well.

As I left class, I had a thought. Mr Trout knew exactly what he was doing. He actually had a good sense of humour, and he was putting on an act. He thought that would make class less boring. He probably practised that pencil-behind-the-ear routine in the staff room. Dollies One and Two coached him.

That *had* to be it. Why else would anyone act so strange?

I believed that theory for about one and a half minutes. Then I let myself forget about Mr Trout and think about more important things.

Like the Sixth-Grade Follies finance committee. We were scheduled to meet after school, to talk about which charitable organizations we might want to donate our proceeds to. I was going to suggest this theatre group in Stamford that trains hearing-impaired actors and puts on plays with sign-language accompaniment. (I had learned about them from the family of one of my favourite charges, Matt Braddock, who is profoundly deaf.)

I ended up seeing Mr Trout twice more that day. The first time, I was rushing to lunch after gym. As I raced round a corner, I spotted him a few metres in front of me.

I slowed down. No way would I let him see me. What could I possibly say to him— "Er, nice class today?"

Here's what I noticed, walking behind Mr Trout. He stayed close to the wall. He had no bounce in his step at all. His hair sat on his head like a helmet. (I wondered if he used hair spray.)

At the canteen door, a group of three teachers was chatting away. One of them, Mr Dougherty, smiled at Mr Trout as he passed, and nodded hello.

Mr Trout must not have noticed. He walked right past without even looking in the teacher's direction. Mr Dougherty just shrugged and plunged back into the conversation.

I think Mr Trout needed to learn some manners. Oh, well. He was new. And shy, maybe. No big deal.

I slipped into the canteen and joined the lunch queue.

The second time I saw Mr Trout was just before last period. I happened to pass the staff room when I heard peals of laughter. I glanced inside to see four or five teachers sitting at a table, doubled up at something Mr Williams was saying. I was dying to listen. They all looked as if they were having a great time.

That was when I noticed Mr Trout. He was at another table, reading a book, facing away from the other teachers. As Mr Williams went on, Mr Trout hunched tighter over his book.

Now, I'm sorry, but *that* was weird in a major way. It wasn't just shy. It wasn't just bad manners, either.

I think Mr Trout needed his own Short Takes course. In Human Relations.

After school I raced to my locker. I threw my books in and began pulling out what I needed to take home.

I was so wrapped up in thinking about the Follies, I almost didn't notice the conversation next to me.

Sanjita, Maria and Sandra were at *their* lockers, not far from mine. They were giggling about something.

Before I closed my locker, I heard Maria say, "Of course it is! It's the most obvious one in the world!"

"You think so?" Sandra asked.

"I know so!" Maria insisted. "My uncle wears a toupee just like the Trout's. Haven't you noticed the grey hairs *just along the bottom*, where his real hair begins?"

"And how it never, ever bounces or falls across his face?" Sanjita added. "It's really unnatural."

"I don't know," Sandra said. "It's a weird style and all, but it looks real to me."

"When was your last eye examination?" Maria asked.

"Ha ha," Sandra replied.

"There's got to be some way we can find out," Sanji said.

"We could ask him," Maria suggested.

5th CHAPTER

"Where are the pretzels?" I called out.

"I'll get them!" Becca replied.

She ran out of the kitchen. I dumped some crisps into a bowl and reached into the fridge for a bunch of grapes. I added them to a fruit bowl that already had apples, oranges and bananas.

I looked at the spread on the kitchen worktop—plain crisps, tortilla crisps, fruit, M & M's, biscuits and (soon) pretzels. "Do you think this'll be enough?" I asked Mama.

"For seven sixth-graders?" Mama said. "I'll give it half an hour. But don't worry. Daddy's outside cleaning the barbecue."

It was 9:45 on Saturday morning, fifteen minutes before a meeting of the Follies performance committee. We'd already begun working on the script at school. Our title was *Hooray for Stoneybrook!* In our "plot", SMS is really a school for celebrities in disguise.

This was our first meeting at my house. I was petrified. I wanted so badly to make a good impression.

Becca came rushing into the kitchen with a huge, open bag of pretzels. "Here!"

"Where were they?" Mama asked her.

"Oh . . . in my bedroom." She quickly added, "*Squirt* brought them there!"

"Uh-huh! Young lady, what are you going to do when your brother's old enough to defend himself?"

Becca ignored Mama's comment. "Jessi, do you want me to tape the meeting?"

"Tape it? Why?" I said.

"So you won't forget your ideas!" she replied. "Or I could just, like, listen and help out if you forget anything."

Oh, boy! Becca Ramsey, show-biz brat in the making. "You can listen if you help me get things ready."

"Yeeeeaaaa!" Becca grabbed two bowls and ran into the living room.

We were ready by 9:57. At 10:03, the doorbell rang.

"I'll get it!" Becca screamed.

We both got there at the same time. Becca pulled the door open and said, "Hi! I'm Jessi's sister!"

It was Randy Rademacher, a boy I didn't know too well. His dad was standing with him.

"Hi," Randy said.

Randy's dad was looking around the living room, hardly noticing my sister and me. "Are your parents at home?" was the first thing he said.

Luckily, Mum came walking in at that moment. "Hello, there," she said sweetly. "I'm Jessi and Becca's mother. Nice to meet you."

Mr Rademacher smiled and put out his hand. He looked relieved. "Hello, I'm Bill Rademacher. You have a lovely home."

"Thank you," Mum replied. "You're welcome to stay if you'd like. My husband's in the garden preparing the grill."

"Oh, the kids'll be having lunch?" Mr Rademacher asked.

"Yes, and we have plenty of burgers and hot dogs, so don't be shy."

"That's nice of you, but I've got some errands." He backed out of the door. "Phone me when you're ready, son."

Randy sank onto the living room sofa. He seemed a little nervous. Just as his father had seemed.

I offered Randy some crisps and sat opposite him.

"Am I the first one?" he asked.

"Uh-huh," I said. "But everyone's coming."

"Except Mara," Randy said. "I saw her in front of her house."

"Oh? Is she feeling all right?"

He shrugged. "She looked fine. She said she had to go to the mall with her mum."

"Uh-huh."

I didn't ask any questions. Mara Semple's OK, but her parents were awfully cold to us when we moved in.

I mean, I know it's not right to judge, and maybe Mara really did have something important to do. But people can be weird. It's hard to believe, but some people are very uncomfortable about being in African-Americans' houses. Uncomfortable? Scared is more like it sometimes.

Like Mr Rademacher. He was being so wary when he was at the door. What did he expect to see?

I don't know. The whole thing is very unfair and very confusing.

Luckily, kids are usually much more easy-going than parents. Randy, his mouth full of pretzels, was reaching into his rucksack. "I've got this great idea," he said.

Ding-dong!

"I'll get it!" Becca yelled.

During the next few minutes the rest of the committee arrived (minus Mara). Each one was greeted by our honorary mascot, my sister.

Randy was dying to show us something. He pulled some sunglasses, a comb, a small pillow, a toy microphone and a box of raisins out of his bag. "Can I use your bathroom?" he asked.

"Of course." I showed him where it was, and he disappeared inside for about five minutes.

When he came out, his hair was slicked back and he was wearing the sunglasses. He'd tucked the pillow under his shirt, and he was holding the toy mike. He flashed us a smile.

Between his front teeth was a huge gap. It took me a couple of seconds to realize it was part of a raisin, smushed into the crack.

"Mr Williams . . . as Elvis!" he shouted. Then he began wiggling and singing an off-pitch version of "Jailhouse Rock".

Well, we *screamed*. Mr Williams does have slick hair, a pot belly and a tooth gap. And he has that smooth, Elvis-style voice.

Next Bobby Gustavson gave me a script he'd been working on, based on *Wayne's World*. He played Wayne—and guess who volunteered to play Garth?

Me.

OK, it wasn't typecasting. But it was hilarious.

We tried out a couple of other ideas, and pretty soon we were rolling on the floor. Aunt Cecelia came in at one point and asked us if we'd gone out of our minds.

Randy took her hand and sang "I'm All Shook Up" as Elvis—and she actually *danced*! Wow! I've never seen Aunt Cecelia loosen up *that* much.

Then, at midday, Daddy came in and said, "Barbecue's ready! Come and get it!"

You never saw a crowd of kids stand up so fast.

On our way to the back door, Randy said, "Miss Bernhardt and Miss Vandela are going to die when we show them this."

Then it hit me. The Perfect Idea. I didn't know why no one had thought of it before. I stopped right in the kitchen.

"The two Dollies!" I exclaimed. "We have to get some Dolly Parton wigs!"

"Yeah! And some, like, gigantic bras," suggested another committee member, Jamie Sperling, her face turning red.

"Here's the main plot: the Dollies are trying to put on the Sixth-Grade Follies," Randy said, "just like in real life—only the school is full of celebrities."

"The Folly Dollies!" exclaimed Justine Moss, who was also on the committee.

"Elvis darlin', y'all just have to tra out fuh the show," I drawled.

"Jessi, you've got to be one of them," Jamie said. "That would be *so* hilarious."

A black Dolly Parton? I suppose that would be funny. Did I want to be laughed at because of that? Well. . .

"Maybe," I replied. "Unless they insist on playing themselves."

We chattered away as we walked out to the garden. Becca tagged along behind us, grinning like crazy.

If I didn't know better, I'd think she wanted to be in the show.

Well, she had three years to prepare. No harm in starting early.

Daddy's barbecue was amazing. We ate till we could hardly move.

My parents insisted on a preview of the show, which we gave them. They thought it was great.

I hoped the Dollies agreed.

6th CHAPTER

Sunday

Jessi and I sat for my brothers and sisters today, and Becca came along.

Eight kids. And then we had visitors. What a job. Good thing you recovered from your mono, huh, Mal? You would not have believed how well Mal controlled the chaos.

Uh, Jessi, I'm supposed to be the one who makes up the stories.

It's not a story. It's just a — you know...

An embellishment.

Right.

A *big* embellishment. But I had to do it. Kristy *makes* us write in that BSC notebook. I couldn't just tell the truth about our job. No one would believe it.

Let me begin at the beginning.

You know how it is to sit for siblings. No matter how wonderful they are, they always fight about something. Food, toys, tapes, TV programmes, whatever. With three siblings, it's even worse. Four? Forget it.

Now try to imagine seven.

That's what it's like in the Pike house, twenty-four hours a day. You've heard of the Seven Dwarfs? Well, Mal's brothers and sisters are the Seven Terrors: Chaos, Disaster, Ruckus, Racket, Pandemonium, Turmoil and Noise.

I usually take a foghorn and a shield when I sit for them.

OK, I'm exaggerating (a bit). They're actually great kids. Besides, Mr and Mrs Pike always make sure they have two sitters. And Mal's usually one of them.

I was getting ready to go over there the day after the Follies committee meeting at my house. I was in a fabulous mood.

It's a good thing I was. Otherwise my sister would have driven me crazy—even *before* I went to the Pikes'.

I was still in my pyjamas when she ran into the kitchen. "Are you leaving yet?"

53

"No, silly," I said with a laugh. "Not dressed like this."

"Oh. Oops! Can I go with you?"

I took a box of cereal from the cabinet. "Well, I don't know if Mr and Mrs Pike would want that—"

"They would! They like me."

"I know they do, Becca. But when they're away from home—"

"Can't you phone them? *I'll* phone them! I need someone to play with today!"

I gave a sigh. "What about going over to Charlotte's house? (Charlotte Johanssen is Becca's best friend.)

"She's going to her grandparents'."

"All right," I said. "I'll call the Pikes as soon as I've finished."

Becca's face lit up. "All *right*!"

Now, only Nicky Pike is Becca's age, and he hates girls. Becca's friendly with his sisters, but not exactly best buddies.

So why was she so excited? I didn't know. But Becca was excited about a lot of things these days. Maybe she was going through a phase. And I suppose the idea of a weekend afternoon without a playmate must have seemed pretty awful.

I did phone Mr and Mrs Pike. They said they were happy to have her come over. And my parents agreed, too.

That was how I ended up walking

to Mal's house with Becca the Jumping Bean.

She didn't stop asking questions.

"When are your auditions for the Follies?"

"Monday, after school," I replied.

"*After school?* Can I watch?"

"Sorry, Becca. It's for sixth-graders only."

"Can you do that singer's voice again?"

"You mean Dolly Parton?"

"Yeah."

"Not in the street!"

"Please?"

By the time we got to the Pikes', I was singing "Nine to Five" in my best Dolly Parton voice.

Becca was cracking up. Neither of us noticed Nicky and Claire Pike at the side of the house.

But they noticed me.

"You stink," was Nicky's greeting to me.

I immediately stopped singing. "A-hem! Thank you."

Nicky's eight. He thinks everything stinks, except karate and whatever else boys at that age like.

Claire, on the other hand, is five. She thought I was great. "More! More!" she insisted.

Mr Pike put his head round the front door. "Hello, girls!"

"Hi!" Becca and I called out.

Crassshhh!

"Er, excuse me." Mr Pike ducked back into the house. I heard him yell, "Adam Pike! How many times have I told you not to climb on the kitchen worktop?"

Thump-thump-thump-thump-thump!

"What happened?"

That was Mrs Pike, charging downstairs.

"I'd better go in," I said to Becca.

I ran inside. Mr Pike was picking broken pieces of a bowl off the floor with a dustpan and a sponge. A pool of milk was spreading, where a carton had fallen.

At the table, Jordan and Byron Pike were sniggering at their brother. (Adam, Jordan and Byron are ten-year-old triplets.)

Just beyond the kitchen, the back door swung open. Mallory flew inside, followed by two of her sisters, Vanessa (who's nine) and Margo (seven).

The three of them spoke at once:

"Hi, Jessi!" said Mal.

"Becca!" cried Vanessa.

"Adam, you're such a clot!" exclaimed Margo.

Adam lunged at Margo with the dustpan. "Rrrraagghhh!"

"Stop!" Margo shouted. She stepped in

the milk puddle and fell.

Jordan howled. "Who's the clot?"

Mrs Pike was leaning against the kitchen wall, shaking her head. "Welcome to the madhouse, Jessi," she said.

Needless to say, the Pike parents left within minutes (with relieved smiles on their faces). Mal and I prepared for the worst.

But the strangest thing happened. Becca took over. Yes, Becca, my little nuisance sister.

"Let's go outside," she suggested.

"Nahhh," Byron said. "I want to work on my model."

"OK." Becca sighed. "Too bad you'll miss out on all the fun."

"What fun?" Byron looked sceptical.

"You won't know unless you come with us," Becca replied.

Mal and I followed them out. We took a couple of garden chairs and put them in the sun. It was one of those perfect, cool days when the sun feels just right.

"Jessi," Mal said, "you must read this new book. It is so cool. . ."

We gossiped and chatted, chatted and gossiped. I don't know how long it was before the revelation hit us.

We had actually had an entire conversation without one interruption.

Not one complaint. Not one injury.

We looked over towards the garage. Becca and the Pikes were huddled in a circle, talking. Margo was laughing hysterically about something. Adam had that *boy* look—you know, that sneer that says, "I'm not interested at all. Tell me more!"

"What are they doing?" Mal asked.

"Let's move closer," I suggested.

Trying to look casual, we picked up our chairs and put them back down within earshot of the group.

Becca whispered something. All of them moved to the farthest corner of the garden.

Before long, Carolyn and Marilyn Arnold wandered by. (They're twins who live in the neighbourhood.) "Hi!" Marilyn called out. "What're you doing?"

Becca waved them over. "Come on!"

Mal and I talked some more. When the kids all darted into the front garden, we shrugged and followed them.

We saw the triplets racing off down the street.

"Hey!" Mal called out. "Where are you going?"

"To the Barretts'!" Adam replied.

"Matt and Haley's!" Jordan and Byron called out. "To invite them over!"

Now, the triplets *are* ten, and those

families are all in the neighbourhood—but this was too sneaky for comfort.

"Thanks for asking," Mal snapped.

"Sorry," Adam shouted. "We'll be right back."

A few minutes later, the triplets returned, together with Buddy and Suzi Barrett, and Matt and Haley Braddock. Twelve kids altogether!

But do you know what? Becca had them enthralled. Mal and I had no idea what she was doing. When we were inside, they went out. When we were out, they went in.

We kept hearing giggles though. And we didn't have to do a thing apart from pouring an occasional glass of apple juice.

It was the easiest sitting job I'd had in a long time. And I began wondering if the BSC would accept Becca as a *junior*-junior member.

A sitter-in-training, maybe? She could accompany me on all my jobs.

Mal laughed at the idea. She said the day was a total fluke. Next time they'd be at each other's throats.

Oh, well, it was worth a thought.

7th
CHAPTER

When I walked to school on Monday, there was a tennis ball in my throat.

Well, that was what it felt like. Big and scratchy and *stuck*.

"Hrrr . . . hrrr," I grunted.

"Jessi, we're approaching school," Claudia said. "Please behave yourself. If you spit on the pavement while everyone's watching us, I swear I'll never speak to you again. You sound as if you're about to spit your guts out."

Thank goodness Mary Anne the Kind and Generous was with us. She said in a concerned voice, "Are you feeling all right, Jessi?"

"Fine," I said. "Just a little sore throat."

Throat infection. Mumps. Pneumonia. Those were the words that flew through my brain.

But I tried to block them out. Today was a big day. First of all, I was going to help run auditions for the Follies.

Second of all, I was going to audition, myself.

I wished the two Dollies hadn't asked us committee members to audition for parts. I mean, they said it was just a formality—but *please*. What if I really blew it?

I knew I'd do well in the dancing department. But we each had to recite something from memory, like a poem or speech. And, worst of all, we had to *sing*.

Do you know what my singing voice sounds like? It peels wallpaper. It makes dogs howl. It makes Jerry Lewis sound beautiful.

OK, I'm going overboard. Once upon a time I thought I was a pretty good singer. But I'd learned the truth about my voice the hard way. Remember I told you about my triumph as the crocodile and the dog in *Peter Pan*? Well, I hadn't auditioned for those parts. I *had* tried out for the role of Peter. I was so sure I'd get it. Sigh!

Ever since then, I've been insecure about my singing. (I still think I might have got the part if only I could carry a tune better.)

And now it didn't help that on my big

audition day a family of glop had decided to rent space in my throat.

"Hrrrrr . . . hrrrr. . ."

We were going into school now. Claudia rummaged in her bag and pulled out a sweet packet. "Here, take one of these."

"What are they?"

"Special lozenges, guaranteed to clear your throat."

I ripped open the packet. It was filled with tiny black pellets. "What do they taste like?" I dumped a few in my hand and popped them in my mouth.

Claudia's eyes grew about three sizes. "No! I said *one*!"

Too late. The troops had landed. I felt as if a small army with liquorice-tipped sabres had invaded my mouth. My sinuses blew open. My eyes swelled with tears.

Mary Anne thrust a couple of tissues in front of me. I put them to my mouth and spat. "Aargh!"

"Are you OK?" Mallory asked.

"Yuck!" I gasped. "These are *horrible*!"

Claudia let out a low whistle of awe. "You won't have another sore throat till you're twenty-seven."

I ran to the nearest water fountain. It didn't help much. The cold water just irritated my throat. I didn't know if I'd ever talk again.

But at least the tennis ball had gone.

"I'm—I'm all right," I lied as I stood up from the fountain.

"Will you be able to sing for your audition?" Stacey asked.

"When I open my mouth I'll knock them out with the liquorice smell," I replied. "They won't be able to hear a thing."

They laughed. We said our goodbyes and headed for the lockers.

Sanjita was at hers, just closing up.

"Hi," I said. (Ooh, those *H* words tickled.)

She gave me a huge smile. "It's all arranged."

"What is?" I asked.

"You know. The toupee thing."

What? said my face.

Sanji sighed with exasperation. "Today's the day we're going to find out if Trout-Man is wearing a rug. Weren't you there when we planned it?"

I remembered that Sanji and a few other kids had been gossiping after class last Monday, but I hadn't joined them.

"I don't think so," I said.

Sanji giggled. "It's *perfect*. We're going to expose him in the middle of class."

"No! You wouldn't."

"Oh, come on, admit it, Jessi. You're dying to know about his hair."

"Well, yes, but isn't this a little . . . mean?"

Sanji's smile disappeared. "Don't do anything to spoil this."

"But Sanji, how could they do something like that?"

"I'm not kidding."

I'd never seen Sanjita so serious. She was glaring at me.

"You know, I didn't have to tell you, Jessi. I trusted you."

What was the use? Class had already got so out of hand. If they didn't do this to Mr Trout now, they'd just try it again some other time.

"OK, OK," I said with a sigh.

I worried through registration. I worried through my first and second classes. I hardly noticed the "good luck" note Mal passed me in class. If I wasn't thinking about the audition, I was thinking about the plot to de-hair Mr Trout.

By Short Takes I was numb. It didn't help that every single person in class was on his or her best behaviour.

Somehow, that was the creepiest thing of all.

People took notes and listened. Everyone was smiling. Mr Trout must have thought he'd discovered the secret to Discipline by

Doing Nothing. He actually tried to crack a joke or two, I think. (I don't know for sure. With him, it was rather hard to tell.)

I had no idea what this plan was. Sanjita hadn't told me. I just sat, expecting the worst.

About halfway through the class, Mr Trout began erasing the blackboard. "All right, I need a few volunteers to write a simpler version of the program we just did." He gestured towards the blackboard. "I'll add two points to your grade-point average if your program has the fewest steps."

Six kids jumped up from their desks. Mr Trout's eyes practically popped out. Suddenly he looked completely different. I realized it was because I was seeing him smile for the first time.

"Er, three at a time, please," he said.

Jimmy, Sandra and John grumbled as they sat down. But they all had these sly little smiles I didn't trust.

Craig began writing on the left-hand side of the board, Renee in the middle, and George on the right. Mr Trout watched over their shoulders carefully.

His back, of course, was to the classroom.

After a couple of minutes, Mr Trout stepped forward, to explain something to Renee. I noticed that Craig and George immediately stopped writing. Both were stepping back from the board, hands on chins, as if they were viewing their own work.

Craig stepped towards the corner, where a long, hooked wooden pole lay against the wall. He took the pole and tiptoed back.

I held my breath. Craig wouldn't do something really stupid, like *hit* Mr Trout. Would he?

He raised the pole high and slipped the hooked end into the handle of a rolled-up world map directly above Mr Trout. As Craig slowly pulled, the map rolled down.

George was pulling something from his pocket that looked like a fish hook. When the map was within reach, he grabbed its handle and clipped the fish hook onto it.

Craig put down the pole gently, as George guided the other end of the fish hook into Mr Trout's hair.

"So you see," Mr Trout said to Renee, "those two steps may be combined—"

My heart stopped. He hadn't noticed a thing.

With a sharp flick of the wrist, George released the map. It slid up into its metal tube with a *smack*.

Dangling from the hook was a limp patch of stiff, black fur.

The room fell silent. I caught a glimpse of shock on Craig's face. I closed my eyes. I couldn't bear to look at Mr Trout.

Then the giggling started. It began with Maria and caught on.

When I opened my eyes, I saw the real Mr Trout.

Wow, did he look different!

He had a ring of greyish-black hair that went up to the level of his ears. Above that, his scalp was as shiny as a pink mirror.

"Well." Mr Trout was blushing. Above him, the toupee was bobbing around like a little lost animal. Craig, George and Renee were gaping at it.

It was horrible. It was cruel. It was the worst prank I could possibly imagine.

But it was hilarious.

Maria was guffawing now. All around me, my classmates were red-faced with laughter. Someone called out "Conehead!"

A laugh started out in my stomach, like a tickle. Then it began to spread through my body. I tried to keep it in, but I couldn't. It exploded out of me like a bomb. I was rocking in my seat, *sick* with laughter.

And then, just when I thought I was getting it under control, Mr Trout began jumping up to try to grab his toupee. It seemed to be avoiding him, squirming out of the way. That just made everybody worse.

At last he managed to grab it. "Well," he repeated, putting it back on his head. "Quite a humorous . . . interlude. You three may sit down."

As Craig, Renee and George went back to their seats, Mr Trout took an eraser and turned to the blackboard.

I collected myself. I reminded myself what a serious situation this was. I tried to think of it from Mr Trout's point of view.

And then I caught a glimpse of something shiny on the back of the toupee.

It was the fish hook, swinging to and fro.

Forget it. The whole class was going, going, gone.

Well, news of the Balding of Mr Trout spread through the school like wildfire. By the end of the day, everybody was talking about it.

My BSC friends wanted to hear every detail. They laughed at my description but agreed the trick was mean. Mary Anne was especially horrified. Kristy insisted that Mr Trout "brought it on himself", and

Stacey couldn't believe he didn't discipline anyone.

We chatted so long, I almost forgot about my audition. Mal was the one who brought it up. By that time it was too late to be nervous.

Everyone wished me luck. Mal ran with me to the school. We hugged goodbye in front of the assembly hall, and I dashed inside. I was determined to be fantastic!

8th
CHAPTER

"Left, right, skip, skip! Arms up, jump . . . again!"

Again?

The gym was packed with sweating sixth-graders. Dolly One, in a skin-tight, neon-striped dance outfit, was leading all the auditioners in a dance routine.

The truth? It was more like an exercise class for the aerobically challenged.

March a little one way. March a little the other way. Hands up, hands down. Clap. Jump.

Ho-hum!

I knew a lot of the kids around me. In real life, they were perfectly well-coordinated. They could walk and talk at the same time. But here on the gym floor, they were transformed. It was as if their legs and arms had declared war on them.

70

I had never seen so many eleven-year-olds get their left and right confused.

OK, OK, I *know* it sounds snobby. But I was used to ballet class with Mme Noelle, who has a fit if your *demi-plié* is too *grande* for her taste.

(I don't even think she knows what the word "skip" means. She would be going crazy if she were here. "Skeep?" she would say. "What eez zees *skeep*? Zees ees not *donce*!")

But I skipped. And I reached. And I stepped. And when I got too bored I helped a couple of my friends.

When it was over, Dolly Two taught us a song.

I remembered it from the video of last year's Follies. It was called "At SMS", and it was set to the tune of "Under the Sea" from *The Little Mermaid*:

At SMS the teachers cheer,
Because they won't have us next year.
We'll have it made
In seventh grade
At SMS. . .

We all knew the tune, and the lyrics were funny. So it was pretty easy to learn.

But I wasn't exactly thrilled with the squawks that came from my mouth. I think Claudia's lozenges had made me even worse, if that were possible.

71

"All right, that sounds terrific!" Dolly Two called out. "Now let's try putting together the song and the dance."

Half the group cheered. The other half looked petrified. Me? I fell in between.

The two Dollies started the music again. I leaped into the dance routine. And I sang at the top of my lungs.

Alone.

Well, that was what it felt like. All the loudest singers suddenly got laryngitis when they had to dance at the same time.

My voice echoed through the gym like a police siren. I was *mortified*. I thought the windows would crack.

I put my hand over my mouth and said, "Oops!"

Dolly Two was smiling. "That was great, Jessi! Don't stop."

I tried. Honestly I did. But now I felt as if someone had put a twist-tie around my vocal cords. The police siren became a mouse squeak.

Very attractive.

It took a few run-throughs, but finally some other kids did start singing along.

"OK, time for groups!" Dolly One called out. "We'll divide you into fours, so we can really see how you're doing. We'll be helping you out, so don't worry if it's not perfect."

72

She went through the gym, dividing us up.

As about sixty people had turned up, that meant fifteen groups.

Mine was third. Nice and early.

I didn't make any mistakes. My voice didn't straighten out Dolly One's curls. I kept a smile on my face.

All in all, I was happy.

While the other groups danced, the rest of us waited in the seats. We performance committee members sat near the Dollies' table. We had all helped organize the auditions—signing people in, putting names in alphabetical order, things like that. But now there was nothing left to do, except sit and get nervous about what came next.

I wanted so badly for Mal to be there—or *any* of my BSC friends—but the Dollies had decided on a "No Friends" rule. They thought too many people would make the auditioners nervous.

They were probably right, but I really could have done with some moral support.

When all the groups had finished, Dolly Two announced, "Now comes the hard part, kids – the individual audition. You will have a chance to sing a song *or* recite your memorized material."

Everyone just stared at her. We looked

like the Zombies from Planet X.

"Look, this isn't an audition for a Broadway show," Dolly Two said warmly. "Remember, you are all *in*. Every single one of you will be in the Follies. These auditions are just to see where your strengths are, and where you need work. Of course we'll select people to speak certain lines, sing a couple of solos—but more importantly, we need a good, big chorus. A chorus that looks as if it's having fun. So just go out there and enjoy yourselves."

"OK, we'll go alphabetically," Dolly One called out. "Ben Abbott!"

Ben raced on to the gym floor. He was so excited he nearly fell. He had nearly fallen during the dance combo, too. Luckily he stayed upright during his speech. He delivered the Gettysburg Address, or something like it, at the top of his lungs:

"FORCE, GORE, AND SEVEN YEARS AGO, OUR POOR FATHER BROUGHT FORTH ON THIS CONDIMENT A NEW NATION. . ."

The Dollies cut him off before we all cracked up (or lost our hearing).

Next Lauren Aronsen sang "Maybe" from the musical *Annie*. That was great.

Jeff Atkinson sang the theme song from *Shining Time Station*. He could have done with a little more coal in his engine.

I heard everything from Shakespeare to sitcoms. A girl called Liz Cohen did the "Vitameatavegamin" routine from *I Love Lucy* (if you haven't seen that episode, you *must*). It was incredibly funny.

But *R* is pretty far into the alphabet. Which meant sitting through a lot of shy performers.

I thought I would turn into a fossil before my turn came. Luckily I had my rucksack so I reached in and took out a book. I got so involved in it I didn't even hear Miss Vandela call my name.

"*Pssst!* Go!"

A girl behind me tapped me on the shoulder.

"Me?" I said, bolting out of my seat.

The Dollies (and all the rest of the auditioners) were staring at me. "Come on down!" Miss Vandela said.

Be a pro, Jessi, I said to myself.

I stood up straight. I smiled. I walked calmly on to the gym floor.

As I approached front and centre, Miss Berndardt exclaimed, "Oh, good! You're doing something from *Maniac Magee*! I love that."

Huh?

I looked down. My right hand was still clutching the book I'd been reading.

"Oops. I was just . . . er, wait a second. . ."

I ran back to the seats and gently tossed the book towards my rucksack. It fell through the seats and slapped on to the floor.

So much for being a pro!

"Actually, I was going to recite 'The Owl and the Pussycat'," I announced.

I'd recited that poem a million times to Squirt. I'd memorized it without even trying, then added some pantomime. Even Becca liked to watch me.

The minute I started, I knew I'd picked the wrong thing. In front of eleven-year-olds, I felt a little stupid.

But hey, I was a pro! I put all my energy into it.

The Dollies seemed to like it all right. But they started whispering to each other in the middle of it.

When I'd finished, Dolly One said, "Very nice reciting. Jessi, can you sing for us?"

"*S-sing?*"

Thook!

The tennis ball was back. It just popped up from my stomach and lodged in my throat.

"Yes," Dolly One said. "Anything.

'Happy Birthday', even. If you don't mind. We just want to hear you."

Hadn't they heard enough of me during the group number? Did they want all the auditioners to go screaming for the exits?

I cleared my throat. My tennis ball was turning into a beach ball. My *Peter Pan* audition passed through my mind like an awful nightmare.

I knew one thing for sure. I was *not* going to sing "Happy Birthday".

"Er, can I sing 'I Won't Grow Up' from *Peter Pan*?" (That was the song I *should* have sung at my other audition, instead of "I'm Flying".)

"Of course!" Miss Bernhardt replied.

I swallowed and began:

"I'm never grow up, I'll won't grow up, I don't want to go to tie—"

I stopped. A few kids were trying very hard not to giggle.

"Can I . . . start again?" I asked.

"Jessi, you sound fine," Dolly Two said. "Just relax and do it again."

I did. I made it through the song, and no one threw tomatoes at me.

I can't remember anything about the rest of the auditions. I was in a daze.

At the end, Dolly Two said, "Thank you all—and congratulations! You're the most talented sixth-graders I've seen! This is going to be the best show ever. We'll make all our casting decisions by Thursday, and they'll be pinned up in the main hall."

Everyone started gabbling excitedly. A couple of kids told me they thought I was great. I returned the compliments.

Then, with the rest of the committee members, I helped tidy up. The Dollies were reassuring to all of us. They teased me a little about "I Won't Grow Up" (Dolly Two said, "I'll really liked it!") but they made sure to say I'd recovered beautifully.

After a while, I started relaxing. I knew the show would be fun, no matter what part I landed.

I had to look on the bright side. I'd helped write the show, and I knew for a fact that not one part required a crocodile costume.

9th
CHAPTER

I was flying.

My feet were off the ground. My brain was somewhere between the clouds and Neptune.

I, Jessica Ramsey, was going to play a Folly Dolly. But that's not the best part. At the bottom of Thursday morning's Follies list was this line:

(*Assistant choreographer/dance captain: Jessica Ramsey.*)

Now, I had *hinted* at the idea to the Dollies the week before—you know, "You lot could really use a dance captain to help you out, lah dee dah. . ." That's all. I hadn't wanted to seem pushy, not after my *Peter Pan* experience.

But they had taken me seriously. Yea!

I was in a great mood all day. Even in Short Takes.

Are you wondering what happened to Mr Trout? Well, he went back to wearing his toupee. True to his style, he never said a thing about what had happened.

Since the Great Balding, the class had settled down. Well, sort of. What I mean is, the creativity level of the pranks had peaked. Now it was all downhill. Kids were back to spitballs and note-passing and the usual silly stuff.

So when a note was slipped on to my desk, I wasn't too surprised. I thought it was another "Drop Your Books" command or something.

I opened it up and read:

Dear Jessi,
Please meet me in
the hallway after class.
Important!!!!
Jus

I looked over at Justine Moss. She gave me a shy smile.

Justine is about the last person in the world I'd have expected a note from. She's quiet and studious. But she was on the performance committee, so I thought she had some Follies news.

I waited outside the room after class.

"Come with me," Justine said as she stepped through the door.

I followed her around the corner. She stopped in front of some lockers.

"What's up?" I asked.

She looked as if she was about to burst. "I had a really great idea this morning."

"What?"

"You know that sketch we couldn't work out an ending for—the one where all the celebrities start arguing in the staff room?"

"Uh-huh."

"Well, how about this. Just when things start to get bad, in walks Mr Williams as Elvis. And everyone says, 'I thought you died!' And he says, 'Ah didn't dah, ah wuz kidnapped by Klingons!' You know what a Klingon is, from *Star Trek*?"

"Those ugly bald guys, right?"

"Right. And in walks one with a phaser—and it's Mr Trout!"

"Uh-huh. Well, I don't know. . ."

"Played by *you*, Jessi—in a bald wig!"

"Whoa! Hang on, Jus. I don't mind playing a Folly Dolly, but—"

"It's the same thing, Jessi!" Justine insisted.

"No, it's not."

Justine folded her arms. "I've already told the Dollies, and they thought it was a great idea. Besides, look what we have already. One person is playing Mr Williams with a pot belly. You're doing a Folly Dolly with a wig and a stuffed blouse. . ."

She went on and on. One of our teachers, Mr Jazak, wears Coke-bottle glasses—and we'd written a part for someone with plastic Coke bottles sticking out of his glasses. One sixth-grader was going to portray our woodwork teacher as Pigpen from "Peanuts", only with sawdust falling wherever he goes, instead of dirt. Another kid was going to play our music teacher, Mrs Pinelli, bursting into song with a terrible operatic voice every time she spoke. Stuff like that.

"I suppose we're really going overboard, aren't we?" I said.

"Going overboard is the whole point, Jessi. Remember last year's video, when it showed the audience? The teachers were hysterical!"

"Do you think *Mr Trout* will laugh at himself?" I asked.

Justine sighed. "Look, I don't like it when everyone's unkind to him either. But the Follies is the opposite of unkind. It's showing the teachers how much we like

them. It's like saying, 'You're one of us.'
And the toupee isn't a *secret* or anything.
Everybody knows about it now. Besides,
I've already mentioned the idea to Miss
Bernhardt, and you know what *she* said?
'You lot are so sweet to include him!'"

Rrriiinnnng!

"Oops!" I started to run to my fourth
class of the day. "We'll talk later!"

"Think about it!" Justine yelled.

"I will!"

I did, too. But I still wasn't convinced. In
fact, when I went to the rehearsal after
school, I was all ready to tell Justine I'd
decided against it.

"OK, places for the *Wayne's World*
number!" Dolly One announced the
moment I walked in.

I quickly sat down to watch. Bobby
Gustavson and another boy played Wayne
and Garth in an SMS class, giving idiotic
answers and making total chaos. Jamie
Sperling played the teacher, Miss Flood,
who speaks with an Australian accent. She
kept calling Bobby "Woin".

Then, when the entire cast had arrived,
Miss Bernhardt put us all through our big
production number—and she let me help
out with the choreography.

Next we split into two groups. Miss
Bernhardt went off to the back of the hall to

work on some smaller sketches, while Miss Vandela directed the staffroom sketch. First, she described Justine's idea to everybody, then commanded, "OK, Elvis and Klingon in the wings. The rest of you, places!"

"Er, Miss Vandela," I called out.

I was all prepared to tell her my decision about not playing Mr Trout, but another student was already bending her ear about something.

I climbed on stage. Randy Rademacher, who was playing Mr Williams/Elvis, grinned at me. He was wearing his '50s shades and was combing his hair back. "Wuzz up, Trout-Man?" he asked in his Elvis voice.

Justine ran up to me, holding a flopped brown piece of Latex. "Here, try this on."

"Er, well—" I began.

Randy burst into hysterical laughter. "Look at that! A bald cap!"

Now everybody was looking at me. I held out the limp cap to Justine. "Sorry, I can't—"

"Come on. . ." Justine urged.

"Let's see! Let's see!" Randy said.

"It's just a joke!" someone yelled from on stage.

Mara Semple was in the sketch, too— Mara, the girl who wasn't allowed to visit my house. I could see her rolling her eyes and mumbling to the girl next to her.

Miss Vandela was now looking at us curiously. "Is something wrong?"

I took a deep breath. Here's what went through my mind:

It was *one* imitation.

It wasn't the worst.

It wasn't the longest.

If Mr Trout could take the Balding without losing his temper, he wouldn't mind this—especially if *all* the other teachers were laughing at their own imitations.

I didn't want to blow it. It had taken me a long time to feel *accepted* at SMS. Everybody seemed to respect my talents. They wanted *me* to play Mr Trout, even though I was the wrong sex and skin colour.

Besides, if I chickened out, the Mara Semple types wouldn't let me forget it.

That's showbiz, I said to myself.

I stretched out the latex cap and put it on my head. In my usual ballerina style, my hair was pulled straight back, flat against my scalp. The wig snapped right into place.

"Er, now then," I said in a nasal Trout voice. "Has anyone seen my, er, hair?"

The whole hall went up. *Roared.* Even Mara was cackling.

You know what? It felt great.

Then Randy started singing, "You ain't nothin' but a Chrome Dome, shinin' all the time!"

"Is someone writing this down?" Miss Bernhardt called out.

Two kids grabbed their clipboards.

Randy and I were a real hit. We went on improvising for a few minutes. Miss Vandela was weeping with laughter.

We had practically a whole new sketch—and the last thing Miss Vandela said before we all went home was, "You two are going to steal the show."

Afterwards, the finance committee all walked to my house for its final meeting. The whole way, we couldn't stop talking about the sketch.

The rehearsal had run late, and Mama and Daddy insisted on giving the entire committee dinner. At the table, we told everyone about the Elvis/Klingon routine.

Then I put on the bald wig. Well, I thought Becca was going to have a heart attack. I've never heard that girl laugh so much.

When dinner was over, the committee went into the living room and compared notes. Each of us had contacted possible organizations and asked for information.

Many of the groups had sent brochures.

We talked about them all. We passed some of the materials around. We discussed the causes we liked the most.

And guess what? At the end of the meeting, I proudly printed on the draft of our official programme. "The proceeds from the Sixth-Grade Follies will be donated to the Stamford Theatre for the Hearing-Impaired."

All in all, it had been a great day.

10th CHAPTER

Wednesday

Follies, Follies, Follies. The world is gripped with Follies Fever. Was it _this_ exciting two years ago?

Maybe, but I don't think so. Anyway, I certainly didn't expect the Follies to hold the key to the Mystery of the Baby-sitters Club...

That's Babysitt*ees* Club, as opposed to Babysitt*ers* Club. Stacey made that up. The sittees she was talking about were Becca, Charlotte, Haley, Vanessa and Margo. And the reason for Follies Fever was that *the Sixth-Grade Follies were only two days away*! Between rehearsals, babysitting and ballet classes, the days had whooshed by.

Rehearsals had been going really well, and I had perfected my Mr Trout voice. I was even using the voice in BSC meetings, which drove everybody crazy.

But more about that later. Back to Stacey and the Great Mystery.

Actually, she was only supposed to sit for Charlotte that afternoon. It was pouring outside, so Stacey made sure to bring along her Kid-Kit full of puzzle books, games and art supplies.

"Anybody at home?" Stacey called through the back screen door of the Johanssen house.

"Stacey, come in!" Dr Johanssen said rushing to open the door. "I'll take your wet things."

As Dr Johanssen bustled away with Stacey's raincoat, Charlotte came into the kitchen (which is just off the back entrance).

"Hi, Stacey," she said.

"Hi!" Stacey replied. "What a day!"

"It stinks. I wish it didn't have to rain."

"I've brought a new book of word games."

"Have you?"

"And crosswords, and felt-tip pens."

"Good."

"'Bye, girls!" Mr Johanssen called out as he and his wife flew by. They were on their way to an important meeting. "There are plenty of snacks in the fridge."

Charlotte followed them to the front door. She kept looking out of the window after they'd left.

And looking.

"Charlotte, are you OK?" Stacey asked.

"Yes. Fine."

Something was wrong. Charlotte was hardly ever this quiet. And no one knows Charlotte better than Stacey. The two of them call each other "almost sisters". Everyone says that Char used to be painfully shy until Stacey brought her out of her shell.

"Well," Stacey said in her most cheerful voice, "I think crosswords are perfect for a rainy day."

But just as Stacey reached into the Kid-Kit, Charlotte ran to the door. "Hi!" she screamed as she pulled it open.

"*Hi!*" squealed two voices.

Stacey looked out of the window to see

Margo and Vanessa running across the soggy lawn. The Pikes' estate car was pulling out of the drive.

"I didn't know you were having visitors," Stacey said.

"Well, I am," Charlotte replied with a big smile.

"Er, do your parents know?"

"Hm, I think I forgot to tell them. Please, Stacey. Please can they stay?"

"Please please please please please!" Margo squealed.

"OK."

Now, Stacey didn't *mind* the extra kids, of course. But the secrecy was a little odd, especially from Charlotte.

It was even odder when Haley Braddock appeared at the front door in her mac.

And a few minutes later, Becca Ramsey.

Yes, my family was involved in this, too. Becca had told my parents that Char had invited her, and that it was all right with the Johanssens.

Either Charlotte or Becca was being a little sneak.

Needless to say, the crosswords stayed in the Kid-Kit.

"We're going into the playroom, OK?" Char said to Stacey.

"OK."

Stacey followed them, but when Char got

91

to the door, she announced, "Kids only. This is top secret."

"No problem."

Cool! Stacey knows kids. They love things like that.

She went into the living room and found some magazines to read.

After a *Vogue*, a *New York* and a stab at *Journal of the American Medical Association* (yawn), Stacey's mind started to wander.

Giggles were wafting in from the playroom.

And music, from a tape recorder.

And singing.

Hmmm.

Stacey put down the magazine and wandered closer to the playroom. She heard Vanessa singing the *Sesame Street* song, ending with the words, "Won't you smell my Sesame Feet?"

"Urgh!" the others screamed, giggling like crazy.

OK. Silly songs. Maybe they were embarrassed. That's why they didn't want Stacey to hear.

Back to the living room. A little homework, a cup of tea, listening to children's laughter and raindrops. What an easy job.

All of a sudden, Haley came running in, all excited.

"Stacey, is Kristy the chairman of the

Babysitters Club?" she asked.

"Yes."

"And what are you?"

"Treasurer."

"And Claudia's vice chairman?"

"Right. Why do you want to know?"

"Er, we were arguing about it, that's all."

"Oh."

Exit.

More screaming. Louder music. Stacey was going crazy. She couldn't concentrate.

Then, suddenly, the noise stopped.

A minute later, all five girls came charging into the room. "Were we too loud?" Charlotte asked.

"Well . . . no," Stacey lied.

Haley looked worried. "Did you hear what we were saying?"

"No."

"Oh, good," Charlotte said. "We're going to work on something else now. Something quiet."

"But it's still secret," Margo warned.

"Fine," Stacey said.

The girls bolted from the living room. They ran frantically around the house, giggling. Stacey could hear drawers opening and closing. Through the living room archway she saw Charlotte heading for the playroom with glue and scissors.

"Don't come in till we say it's OK!"

Vanessa shouted from inside.

"I won't!" Stacey answered.

Well, she waited. And waited. Stacey finished her homework. She could hear occasional rips, snips and giggles.

At 5:15 she began packing up. Mr and Dr Johanssen were due back and Stacey had to go to a BSC meeting.

At 5:17 the Johanssens arrived. Stacey explained about Charlotte's visitors.

At 5:19, when Stacey was heading for the door, the girls came barging into the living room.

"Wait!" Charlotte said. "Take this!"

She handed Stacey a huge, handmade envelope that looked like this:

"Wow! What's this?" Stacey asked.

"It's for the whole Babysitters Club," Charlotte explained.

"But don't open it till *everybody's* there," Vanessa insisted. "It's *important*."

For about the hundredth time, Stacey

nodded seriously and said, "OK."

Stacey couldn't wait to open it. But she did exactly what the kids had wanted.

As it turned out, Stacey was the last to arrive at the meeting. "Order!" Kristy boomed as Stacey walked through the door.

"Burger, medium rare!" Logan Bruno replied. (He *always* says things like that when he comes to meetings.)

"Not funny, Bruno," Kristy muttered.

"Maybe you should say something else to open meetings, Kristy," Claudia suggested. "Like . . . I don't know, 'Yabba dabba doo!'"

Everybody laughed. "It's five-thirty," Kristy shouted. "*Yabba dabba doo!* I like it!"

"Wilmaaaaaa!" Logan bellowed in a horrible Fred Flintstone imitation.

"OK, enough!" Chairman Kristy snapped. "Any new business?"

Stacey held out the letter. "This is for us, from Charlotte and her friends."

She showed it around. Everyone leaned forward. "Open it," Mary Anne urged.

Stacey ripped it open and read it aloud:

Priv at invitation!!
Come one come all
to THE WORLD FAMOUS
BSC FOLLYS!!!!!!
One day only!!
A week from Saturday!!!
AT CHARLOTTES' HOUSE
Rsvp Write away
555-8479

"The BSC Follies?" Shannon said.

"How sweet!" Mary Anne exclaimed.

I laughed. No wonder Becca had been so interested in finding out about the Follies! (I learned later that she'd thought of the idea.)

"Can I phone them?" Stacey asked.

"OK," Claud said, handing her the phone.

Stacey tapped out Charlotte's number. "Hi, Char, it's your almost sister ... uh-huh ... We loved it! And *we accept!*"

11th CHAPTER

"She's here! Line up for the finale!" Miss Barnhardt bellowed.

Those were the first words I heard as I raced into the assembly hall.

Or, I should say, the first words I could make out.

Everything else was a jumble—screaming, lines being learned, laughter, arguing.

It was magic time!

Well, magic time minus one hour.

Friday had arrived at last. Me? I was a basket case. For days, my mind had been on nothing but the Follies. In ballet class that week, Mme Noelle said my mind was "in zee ozone".

That evening I could hardly touch dinner. My stomach growled as I walked into the hall, but all I could think was: *Did I bring my bald head? Did I bring my dancing shoes? What comes after* chassé *left?*

I was also singing, "Yoo-ee you-ee you-ee you-ee you-ee," up and down a scale. That's something Shannon taught me. It's called a vocalize, and it's pronounced *vocalease*—but it should be called vocal-*hard*, because your lips start to hurt after doing it too much. (Why "you-ee" as opposed to "Me-you", or "P.U.", or "yabba-dabba-doo"? Don't ask me.) Anyway, it's supposed to make you sing better.

Am I making sense? I hope so, because I still get all worked up just thinking about that day.

"Jessi?"

I became aware of Miss Vandela's voice in the middle of a "yoo" on the way to an "ee".

"Huh?" I said.

"Er, the kids are lining up for the dance finale. I'd like one run-through while we have time. Will you lead them?"

"Yes."

It was a good idea. We'd had a dress rehearsal for the finale the day before, and it had been, well, interesting.

Oh, OK, the truth. It had been *horrible*.

The complete cast was in the finale. And I mean everyone, including kids whose feet seem to grow roots at the sound of the word "dance".

Now don't get me wrong. This "dance" was not like something at the American Ballet Theatre. Just some loose, hip-hop stuff, followed by a kickline. Simple. Fun.

Here's what happened at the dress rehearsal: Ben Abbott, who had worn his high-top trainers, flung them both into the seats during the kickline. Sarah Green had got so nervous she had to go away and be sick. And Ashley Bedell had stormed off-stage, saying the routine was too hard.

Well, Ben, Sarah and Ashley were all there on Friday, raring to go. (And Ben was wearing tightly tied running shoes.)

Dolly Two, who was our piano accompanist, looked at me patiently. "OK, places for the finale!" I shouted.

Everybody scrambled into place. Dolly Two began the intro. I counted out the correct number of beats, then shouted, "Three and four and *go*!"

Oh, boy!

Ben looked as if he was trying to kick a field goal. A couple of the other boys seemed to be involved in Ninja training. And two of the girls ended up dancing right off into the backstage area.

"Hold it!" I called out. "Stop the music."

I was no longer nervous. It was time for

some serious action. I hopped on stage and demonstrated. I answered questions. I simplified steps.

The second attempt was much better. I watched it sitting next to Miss Vandela at the piano. "Let me do one more run-through," I said.

"That's all the time we have, I'm afraid," she said to me gently. "We have to get ready."

I looked at her. She looked at me.

"Eek!" we both screamed, hugging each other.

I love the Dollies. They're just like two kids.

"OK, everybody gather round!" Miss Bernhardt called out.

We all came to the front of the stage. The Dollies told us how wonderful we'd been. They said this was the best show they'd ever worked on. And. . :

They were going to treat us to ice-cream in the canteen after the show!

"Yea!" everyone yelled.

Then we went to work. The light crew turned the lights on and off a million times. The sound crew kept repeating "testing" over and over, even though we only had two mikes. The costume crew scrambled around backstage with needles, thread and tape-measures.

I went back into the corridor. There, under the bright lights, the make-up people were busy fussing with everyone's faces.

"Jessi?"

I turned to see Mallory waving to me. She was at the end of the corridor, near the lobby. I ran to her. We practically smothered each other with hugs.

"Break a leg!" she said.

"Thanks!" I replied. "Oh, I wish you were in this!"

"No way! I'm going to lead your cheering section!"

We hugged again and I ran back to the make-up table.

I sat next to Jamie Sperling, who was struggling with her blonde wig. She and I were to open the show as the Folly Dollies. (Our wigs were on loan from the high school costume shop.)

I pulled my wig over my head. It fitted perfectly. Then I slathered on the make-up.

Kids were zooming to and fro. A girl carrying light bulbs almost collided with a boy carrying props. Ben was practising the steps for the finale. Three girls were singing the words, to help him out.

It was an absolute, total zoo.

"How do ah look?" Jamie said, standing up in her full Dolly get-up.

"Beautiful," I replied. "And me?"

"Well. . ."

We looked so stupid! It was hilarious.

The clock in the corridor said 7:35. Twenty-five minutes to go. I had to see the audience.

I ran backstage. The noise of the crowd was coming through the curtain, all muffled. I sneaked stage right and peeped out, pulling the curtain aside.

The Pikes were negotiating their seats, making a whole row of people move over. Kristy and her family were sitting right behind them. Claudia was at the back of the hall, chatting to Mary Anne and Logan.

So many people were filing in. The hall was almost half full. In just a little while the lights would dim, and we'd be on our way.

I started to shiver. This was nothing like a ballet performance. No routines, no music to guide me along. Just me, Jamie and the audience. If we did well, they'd laugh. If not . . . well, I didn't want to think about that.

"Pssssst! Jessi!"

I looked down at the front row. Becca was waving to me, grinning from ear to ear. I could tell Mama was trying not to screech with laughter at my outfit.

Daddy didn't see me. He was helping Aunt Cecelia with her coat. She, of course, looked exasperated.

Then, out of the corner of my eye, I saw *him*.

Mr Trout.

He was walking into the hall, alone. His toupee was shiny in the glare of the house lights. He took a seat right at the back, opened up a paperback, and started reading.

Suddenly my stomach felt like a pinball machine. I let the curtain fall in front of me.

All my doubts came rushing back into my brain.

What was I doing?

But I had no time to think about it. The two Dollies were rampaging around in their high heels, yelling, "Clear the stage! Fifteen minutes!"

"Full house, kids!" someone yelled from behind me. "The ticket people say we're sold out!"

The whole cast cheered like crazy.

Sold out! I was thrilled. That meant a nice big cheque to the Theatre for the Hearing-Impaired.

I went back into the corridor, where everybody was still hugging and doing last-minute practising.

Miss Bernhardt called "Ten minutes".

Then "Five".

Then "Places".

Jamie and I met at centre stage. We were too nervous to hug. At last Miss Bernhardt yelled, "Curtain up!"

Nothing happened.

"Pull it the other way!" Miss Bernhardt hissed.

"Oh." The boy pulling the curtain yanked again. The two halves of the curtain parted. Jamie and I faced total darkness. I got ready to speak.

But I couldn't say a word. The audience started *howling*—at our costumes!

I stalled for time, fluffing my hair.

They howled again.

When I finally got round to saying my first line: "Gosh, Miss Vandela, do you think we've got enough talent in this school to have a Follies?" the whole audience answered, "*Yes!*"

We were off and running.

In the Folly Dollies introduction, we pretended it would be too hard to find enough kids who could sing and dance to put on a show.

In the next sketch, Dolly Two (Jamie) went into a gym class, and all the kids burst into a rap song. The *Wayne's World* sketch followed on from that.

The staff room sketch came pretty late in the show. I froze a little, thinking about Mr Trout, there in the audience. As I waited for my cue line backstage, I almost chickened out.

But then I heard Bobby say, "Ah'm not dead. Ah wuz kidnapped by Mr Trout, the Klingon."

I stepped out, bald wig and all, and said, "*Kwingon*. Pwease."

Well, I thought I was going to have to stay there all night. The laughter went on for ever. I couldn't keep a straight face. All the kids on stage were cracking up.

I don't know how we got through the number.

We did, though. Somehow. And before I knew it, the finale had sneaked up on us.

I held my breath. We all lined up on stage, arms around each other's shoulders. To my right was Mara Semple. She gave me a squeeze.

When I looked at her, she was beaming. "You're so talented," she said.

Then the curtain opened. And I danced my heart out. I didn't care if it was too easy, or not really "*donce*". To me, it was just as important as any ballet.

And do you know what? Ben was fabulous. So were Sarah and Ashley. When we got to the kickline, the audience was on its feet, clapping in rhythm. We couldn't even hear the piano.

Everyone kept standing, right through the curtain call. The grown-ups were cheering and saying "Bravo!". I could hear loud screaming from the Pikes' row. Plus a loud whistle, followed by, "Yo, Jessi!" which could only have been Kristy.

I was smiling so hard I thought my face would get stuck.

Afterward, we all raced into the corridor. It was one great hug. I must have said "You were great!" seven hundred times—and I meant every one.

The two Dollies told Jamie and me we were so good, they wanted us to take over their classes.

I saw Mr Williams and Bobby doing an Elvis *duo*.

Mrs Pinelli, our music teacher with the operatic voice, was laughing so much she was *hooting*.

The teachers were such good sports. They really seemed delighted by our imitations. I looked around for Mr Trout, but it was so crowded I couldn't tell if he'd come backstage.

"Jessi Jessi Jessi Jessi!"

Becca practically tackled me. Behind her, Mama and Daddy were beaming. "Did you like it?" I asked.

"You were a star," Daddy said.

"I nearly fell out of my seat," Mama added.

Even Aunt Cecelia had something nice to say. "I was proud of my niece—except one of your teachers would not stop slapping the armrest next to me. Now, funny is funny, but he could have been a little more courteous to his neighbours!"

Leave it to Aunt Cecelia.

"Who wants ice-cream?" I asked.

"Me!" Becca screamed.

We all made our way to the canteen. The entire BSC was waiting there. Every single one of them mobbed me.

Except one.

Claudia was mobbing the ice-cream.

12th CHAPTER

I slept like a log Friday night!

I woke up on Saturday to the ringing of the phone. It was Jamie. We had a screaming-for-happiness contest.

Then Justine phoned. And Randy. And Bobby. And, of course, Mallory.

After Mal's call, I went to the kitchen and chatted to my family. Mama said she hadn't known I had such a "sense of comedy". Daddy repeated his favourite parts of the show, doing imitations of *our* imitations. Becca looked at me all starry-eyed. And Aunt Cecelia came in and complained about her feet.

(Actually she did manage a compliment or two.)

"Who's hungry?" Daddy boomed.

"Me!" we all replied.

He made us a humongous breakfast of

eggs, bacon and toasted bagels. I ate every last crumb. I was *starving*. (I don't know why. I'd stuffed myself with praline fudge ice-cream the night before.)

The nicest part of that morning was a phone call from Miss Bernhardt. When she told me how much money the Follies had raised, I nearly fainted.

"I'd like three students to come with me to Stamford to present the cheque on Monday," she said. "And I want you to be one of them. After all, the organisation was your suggestion."

Wasn't that nice of her? My parents agreed straight away.

I don't know where the rest of the weekend went. I do know that I spent most of it going over every second of the show in my head.

From time to time I thought about Mr Trout. No one had mentioned a word about him after the show or over the phone. I hoped he had enjoyed himself.

He must have. Every other teacher loved the show. Even if you didn't have much of a sense of humour, you couldn't help laughing that night.

I was sure the atmosphere had rubbed off.

Still, I was nervous as I walked to school with Mal on Monday.

The sixth-graders, I must admit, were the centre of attention in the main corridor. Jamie was surrounded by kids who were jabbering about the show. Miss Bernhardt was trying to cross to the administration office, but everyone was stopping her to talk.

"Jessi!"

Jamie rushed up to me. Before long, we were joined by Justine, Bobby and Sanjita.

Yes, Sanji had been at the show, too. And she *adored* the Mr Trout imitation. (Surprised?)

I think we would have chatted away the whole day if the registration bell hadn't rung.

I saw Sanjita again just after our first class. She had that Juicy Gossip look in her eye.

"Jessi, did you hear what happened?" she asked.

"No," I replied.

"Trout's out."

"Huh?"

"He hasn't come to school today. I heard Mr Kingbridge talking about him to Mrs Downey. They don't know where he is. He didn't even phone to arrange for a supply teacher."

My stomach sank. "Uh-oh!"

"He couldn't even stick out the last week

of Short Takes." Sanji giggled. "You really did it, Jessi."

"Yes. I suppose so."

"You ought to be on *Saturday Night Live*. See you!"

Now, Sanjita had meant all that as a compliment (I think). But I felt as if I'd been hit by a bus.

Mr Kingbridge is our deputy head-teacher and Mrs Downey our school secretary. If they said Mr Trout wasn't here, it had to be true.

I had driven him away. I had hurt him so badly he couldn't even phone the school.

On my way to my second class, I started to cry.

I was a mess in class. I couldn't think about anything else. Afterwards, Mal tried to cheer me up, but that was impossible.

Between my second and third classes, the whole school seemed to be talking about Mr Trout.

I heard someone say my sketch had been the last straw. Mr Trout had been fuming underneath, and he finally cracked.

Someone else said he had resigned.

Moved out of town.

Left the state.

Left the country.

Threw his toupee in a river and became a monk.

I didn't find any of this funny. Especially the way some kids were treating me. Their conversations would drop to a whisper as I passed by.

I was petrified of going to Short Takes. What if all the rumours were untrue? What if he was just late? What would I say when he walked into class?

Well, as it turned out, I didn't have to worry on that score, at least. A supply teacher was waiting for us.

For some reason, the first thing I noticed was his hair. Definitely real. Greyish-brown, thinning on top. He was a little overweight and wore glasses and a blue blazer. He looked sort of . . . average.

You know what it's like when a supply teacher turns up. So you can imagine what my Short Takes class was like. They were *already* used to pranks and wisecracks.

Now it looked like April Fool's Day.

"Hey, Kwingon!" Craig Avazian yelled as I entered.

"Yea, Jessi!" Janet O'Neal cheered. "Great job!"

John Rosen let out a whistle. A couple of other kids applauded. Maria Fazio said, "Mr Trout wan away!" and burst out laughing at her own joke.

"All *right*!"

112

A deep voice echoed through the room like a gunshot.

The supply teacher stood up, holding the seating plan in front of him. "Obviously you are not following this plan. So I would like you all to move." Grumbling, everyone got up and arranged themselves according to the plan. Then the supply teacher said, "OK. Mr Rosen, Miss Fazio, Mr Avazian, Miss O'Neal this is Warning One. I give *only* one. Is that understood?"

Silence.

"Now, my name is Mr Bellafatto, and I—"

Maria exploded with giggles. "*Bellafatto?*" she repeated under her breath.

The supply teacher stopped speaking. He looked at her calmly and said, "I will be here tomorrow and the remainder of the week. I give homework assignments. And you, young woman, will have twice as much as the rest of the class."

"But—but I—" Maria spluttered.

Mr Bellafatto picked up some chalk and turned to the blackboard. "Now, I'm here at short notice, but I have an idea what you've been learning, so I'll try to fumble my way through—"

While his back was turned, a huge glob of spitball went flying through the air. It landed with a *splat* in Renee Johnson's hair.

113

"Ugh! Mr Bella—"

"Good shot," Mr Bellafatto said to Craig (I don't know *how* he could have seen him).

Craig squirmed. He laughed nervously.

"So good, in fact, I think you should let the head teacher know how talented you are. Right now."

Craig's jaw hit the ground. "But—but I—"

"Hmm. You and Miss Fazio ought to get together. You have the same vocabulary— 'but, but, but'. Do you know the way to the office, or must I send an escort?"

Craig meekly stood up. His lower lip was quivering as he left the room.

Everyone sat up.

Wow! This man was amazing.

What a difference.

With a smile, he said, "You'll find I'm actually not a bad guy . . . for a teacher." He shrugged. "All I ask is that you show a little courtesy. Are you all right, Miss . . . er . . ." He checked the seating plan again. "Johnson?"

Renee nodded quickly. "Yes."

"Good. Let's get started."

He didn't exactly pick up where Mr Trout had left off. I think he went back to an earlier stage of the curriculum. It was hard to tell.

But it didn't matter. After a few minutes,

I realized that I actually understood what he was talking about. *That* was a change. For a supply teacher, he was pretty good. He explained things clearly, answered questions, and he even cracked a few jokes.

And I wasn't distracted by pranks and notes and whispers. They had stopped. Completely.

When he didn't have to discipline anyone, Mr Bellafatto was basically a funny, ordinary man.

By the end of class, I could sense this *relief* in the air.

It should have felt great. I should have been happy that at last I was understanding computer gobbledygook.

But I wasn't. All I could think about was how I had destroyed poor Mr Trout.

After school I met the two Dollies in front of the school, together with Lisa Mannheim and Tom Block, two other kids on the Finance Committee.

Miss Bernhardt drove us all to Stamford. In the car, I tried to gush about the show with everyone else. When Tom mentioned the Mr Trout sketch, I just smiled and nodded. I didn't want to talk about it at all.

But everyone else did. At one point Lisa asked the two Dollies, "Has anyone heard from him?"

Miss Vandela sighed. "Mr Kingbridge was talking to him on the phone as we were leaving. He didn't sound too happy."

Oh, boy!

When we arrived at the theatre office, the manager and director were delighted to see us. The two Dollies insisted that I present the cheque.

I did. And I have never felt so proud and so rotten at the same time.

13th
CHAPTER

It wasn't just me.

That's what I had decided by Wednesday morning. I had thought about it a million times.

I wasn't the only cause of Mr Trout's troubles. Craig was and Maria was and the whole class was. Of course he had left. Who could have put up with all of that?

But even though I wasn't completely to blame, my sketch had been the last straw. So I felt I had to do something.

Before school, I spotted Miss Bernhardt near my locker. "Hi," I said.

"Jessica! How's the star?"

I shrugged. "OK, I suppose. Er, I was wondering if you'd heard anything about Mr Trout?"

Miss Bernhardt sighed and shook her

head. "Oh, that *man*. He gave Mr Kingbridge such a hard time."

"Really?"

"Well, he didn't give any warning—*nothing*. Just didn't turn up. Mr Kingbridge tried phoning him on Monday morning, but his phone was disconnected. Do you know what it's like to get a supply teacher at two hours' notice—when you're not even sure if the teacher is officially absent? Goodness, after a while Mr Kingbridge thought something terrible might have happened, so he spent the lunch break *driving* to Mr Trout's house. Nobody was at home. No car in the drive."

"Wait," I said. "If his phone was disconnected, how could Mr Kingbridge have been talking to him when we all left for Stamford after school on Monday?"

"Mr Trout called him from a phonebox," Miss Bernhardt replied. "He was at a petrol station somewhere in Vermont. He'd decided he couldn't take it any more. Can you believe that? *Vermont!*"

My eyes started welling up again. "So it *was* the Follies!"

"Sweetheart, if it wasn't that it would have been something else. Honestly, that fellow needed to lighten up a bit. I never so much as got a 'good morning' out of him—

none of us teachers did. Are we so . . . so *unapproachable*?"

I couldn't speak. Miss Bernhardt could see I was upset, and she put her arm round me. "Hey, don't blame yourself. You didn't do anything wrong. If anybody should have been insulted, it should have been *me*! That wig of yours looked like a rat's nest!"

I couldn't help giggling. Miss Bernhardt gave me a squeeze. "Don't worry," was the last thing she said before leaving for her class.

By the third period bell, Mr Bellafatto hadn't arrived for Short Takes. He walked in a few minutes late, with Mr Kingbridge.

"Er, children, I have an announcement to make," Mr Kingbridge said. "Your usual teacher, Mr Trout, has decided to . . . well, to take an unexpected leave of absence. He's . . . er, contemplating going back to graduate school, I believe. For the brief duration of this Short Take segment, Mr Bellafatto will be your official teacher. Please make him feel welcome."

"Yea!" cheered a few students.

Mr Bellafatto took a modest bow.

I couldn't stand it any more. Mr Trout had been here, had gone through such torment, and now—*poof!*—just like that, everyone was going to forget him.

Well, not me.

After class a group had gathered in the corridor, all talking about Mr Trout. Sanjita, Maria and Janet were among them. I heard Sanji say, "What a spoilsport."

"We did it to him, you know," I blurted out. "If we'd been nice to him, he would have stayed."

"How could we be nice to him?" Maria retorted. "He was so weird."

Janet shook her head. She looked confused. "Why did he do that? He was going to get another class in a few days. Besides, you don't just *leave* a job like that, especially without another one lined up."

"Yes," I said. "Now he's not only humiliated, but poor."

No one knew what to say to that. I just walked away.

When school ended I went straight to Mr Kingbridge's office. His door was open, and he was busy at his desk. "Mr Kingbridge?" I said, knocking on the door.

"Come in, Jessi," he replied. "What can I do for you?"

I sat on a chair opposite him. "It's about Mr Trout. I heard what happened."

He nodded. "Don't you be concerned. He's doing fine and I'll send him your regards if you want. I think you'll like Mr Bellafatto—"

"Oh, I know I will. It's just that—well . . .

oh, it's so terrible, Mr Kingbridge. He didn't just walk out on you. We kids drove him out. It's all our fault, most of all *mine*!"

"Why? Because of the Follies sketch?"

"That and a million other things." I described all the pranks, including the Balding. I told him what Janet had said about Mr Trout not having a job now.

Mr Kingbridge nodded thoughtfully.

At last I said, "This is so unfair! I mean, I like Mr Bellafatto, but can't we do something to get Mr Trout back? Can't we give him a second chance? Then, after this week, he may get a nicer class."

With a sigh, Mr Kingbridge leaned back in his chair. "You know, before I went into education, I was a waiter."

Huh? Had he even *heard* me?

"I thought the restaurant business might be interesting," he went on. "But I kept getting fired. I'd muddle up people's food orders. Customers would be furious with me for forgetting to bring ketchup, or extra lemons, whatever—and I would take it all so seriously. Lose sleep over it."

"Well, I suppose you weren't meant to do *that* for a living, were you?"

"No. Leaving that business was the best thing I ever did." He gave me a warm smile. "Don't worry, Jessica. One day Mr Trout will find what he's meant to do. I can guarantee you it won't be teaching sixth grade."

"I . . . I suppose so," I said.

"Look," he said gently, "your class's behaviour was rude and inexcusable. I grant you that. But you didn't make Mr Trout leave. It's not about you, or the other kids. Mostly it's about Mr Trout himself. Understand?"

I nodded. "Thanks."

I thought about it as I got ready to leave. Mr Kingbridge had made sense, sort of, but I still wasn't convinced. If Mr Trout came back, I was sure the class would be nicer to him. Maybe he *was* meant to be a teacher. Maybe he just needed more practice.

I sat down near my locker and drew up a petition that looked like this:

We, the undersigned, request that Mr. Trout be asked back to SMS for a second chance:

_____

_____

_____

_____

_____

Before going home I pinned it on the school notice board.

That night I composed a letter and typed it out:

Dear SMS students,

One of our teachers, Mr Trout, has left school. This happened because his students were unkind to him. Also because he was insulted by my portrayal in the Follies. Now he has no job. I think he should be invited back to teach. Please sign the petition if you agree.

Thank you.

Sincerely,

Jessica Ramsey

By Friday, seven signatures followed mine on the petition. Six were the other members of the BSC. The seventh looked like this:

TWOUT-MAN
the KLINGON

14th CHAPTER

Saturday

Well, I thought nothing could be funnier than the Sixth-Grade Follies (and I really mean that, Jessi). But I'm telling you, when Charlotte and Becca and Buddy and their friends reach sixth grade, watch out!

Just remember, you saw it all first at my house.

None of us knew what the "BSC Follies" would be like. Most of the "actors" in it— Becca, Charlotte, Buddy Barrett, the Arnold twins and the rest—had been to the Sixth-Grade Follies the week before.

I was sincerely hoping I wouldn't see any Klingons.

That morning, Mary Anne was getting ready to go to the Barretts'. She was supposed to sit for Buddy and his two sisters, Suzi and Marnie. (Buddy's eight and mischievous, Suzi's five and sweet, and Marnie is an adorable two-year-old.)

Sometimes Mary Anne likes to take her charges back to her house. It's this old farmhouse, built in 1795, and it has an enormous barn and an even more enormous garden. It's a great place to sit for kids.

But since Buddy and Suzi were starring in the BSC Follies, Mary Anne was planning to take them all to Charlotte's.

Until the phone rang.

"Mary Anne, it's for you!" her dad called from the kitchen.

Mary Anne, who'd been washing up, went over the phone.

"Hello," she said.

"Mary Anne, this is an extra-special emergency!" a girl's voice said.

"Charlotte?"

"Yes. Oh, Mary Anne, it's going to rain!"

Mary Anne looked out of the kitchen window. It was cloudy and grey. "Uh-oh!" she said.

"Can we *please* have the Follies at your house? That way, if it does rain, everybody can go into the barn!"

"Hang on, let me ask."

After some negotiating, Mary Anne got the green light from her dad and stepmum.

And that was how the Official First Annual BSC Follies, produced by Becca Ramsey and Charlotte Johanssen, ended up in the Spier-Schafer garden.

Mary Anne raced over to the Barretts' and brought them to her house. Buddy and Suzi didn't stop giggling the whole way. Marnie looked bewildered.

Next came Charlotte. Then Becca and I arrived.

Before long we had a packed house (packed garden?). All the BSC members were there, as well as the Pikes, Mr and Mrs Arnold, Daddy and Mama, the Johanssens and Kristy's family. Even Aunt Cecelia came (although she looked very disapproving of all the noise).

The sky was clearing up, so the kids decided to perform outdoors. Mary Anne's dad and stepmum rushed in and out of the house with kitchen chairs, folding chairs, plastic cartons, anything they could find.

The actors scrambled around, getting ready. Their "set" was a picnic table with a sheet over it, three chairs and a broken clock on an old card table (borrowed from Mary Anne's barn).

Finally Vanessa Pike shouted out:

"Attention please, attention please!"

Everyone quietened down. The performers (except Vanessa) all disappeared into the barn.

"And now, our intro." Vanessa took a piece of paper from her pocket, unfolded it, and read:

"Welcome to our BSC Follies.

We hope you laugh and have some jollies.

Listen and follow me,

To a meeting of the BSC."

Then she bowed and said, "Thank you."

Wild applause.

"Boo!" Adam called out.

Mr Pike leaned over and told him off. Vanessa stuck her tongue out.

Then, one by one, the kids came out of the barn. First Marilyn Arnold, wearing a visor turned back to front and a jogging suit. "Hi, I'm Kristy!" she said.

"Oh, no. . ." Kristy hid her face as everyone burst out laughing.

Vanessa walked out, carrying a rucksack. She had her hair pulled back and fastened by something that looked like a dog bone.

She pulled out a Milky Way bar, stuffed it in her mouth, and said, "Hi, I'm Claudia!"

"Aargh!" Claudia screamed.

Carolyn followed her, pretending to cry. "I'm—"

Sniff, sniff. "Mary Anne! Boo-hoo-hoo-hoo!"

The *real* Mary Anne went red as a beet.

Buddy shuffled out of the barn, carrying a football. He walked up behind Carolyn with this embarrassed grin on his face. "Aw, it's all right, Mary Anne," he said in a monotone.

"Hi, Logan," Carolyn said. Then she whispered, "*You're supposed to put your arm round me!*"

Buddy scowled. "This is *stupid*!" he said, stalking away.

Vanessa rushed over to him. It took some convincing, but Buddy walked back onto the "set" to a round of applause.

The show was saved.

Next came Margo, holding a bag of carrots. "I'm Dawn. Yummy, this is my dinner."

Becca came out in a tutu—then promptly ran back into the barn. (She's loud at home, but *very* shy in public!) At last she came back out as guess who? (I'll give you a hint: she was walking on her toes.)

Squirt broke loose from Mama's arms and ran toward her, saying, "Baka baka baka!"

When Becca gently handed him back, to a chorus of *"Ah's"* from the audience, he threw a fit!

At last Mama quietened him down, and the rest of the company emerged from the garage: Suzi with fake glasses (as Mal); Charlotte, in a very fancy outfit, as Stacey; and Haley, bouncing out as Shannon, singing "You-ee you-ee you-ee."

Marilyn/Kristy turned the hands of the old clock to five-thirty and screamed at the top of her lungs, *"ORDER! OR ELSE!"*

We were *convulsing*. Snorting with laughter. Kristy was on the ground.

"NOW FOR OUR OFFICIAL THEME SONG!" Marilyn/Kristy barked. *"NOW! COME ON, SING!"*

Then, together, in teeny voices, they sang to the tune of the *Sesame Street* song:

"BSC, that is we,

BSC!"

That was as far as they got before dissolving into giggles.

They started again, and finally reached the "won't you smell my Sesame Feet" punchline. Well, that made them crack up completely.

"What does *that* have to do with

the Babysitters Club?" Jordan Pike complained.

"It was just *funny*, that's all!" Vanessa snapped.

"No, it's not. It's true," Jordan replied. "About your feet."

"*Kids*. . ." Mrs Pike warned.

The show went on. How was it? Well, *crude*. It didn't have much dialogue, and there weren't any more songs.

But it was one of the funniest plays I have ever seen.

Marilyn/Kristy shouted everything she said. At one point she picked up a stick and went to do some batting practice.

Vanessa/Claudia kept stuffing her face the whole way through, constantly pulling snacks out of her rucksack, mumbling all her words. At one point she picked up the clock and said, "This would make a fabulous hat!"

Charlotte/Stacey sniffed disapprovingly. "N.O.M.H—Not On My Head!"

Margo/Dawn crunched on carrots till she began to look sick.

Suzi/Mal pretended to write in a notebook that had MAL'S GRATEST STORY written on the cover. Carolyn/Mary Anne looked over her shoulder and burst into tears every few seconds.

Becca did her imitation of my stretching

exercise, breaking into giggles every time she saw me. And Haley/Shannon's singing began to sound like a coyote.

Then, after whispering something to Vanessa, Margo yelled, "Brrrring!"

Vanessa picked up the phone and said, "Hello, Babysitters Club! Who? The Pike triplets? Sorry, you'll have to call the Monkey-sitters Club."

"Hey!" three voices blurted out.

Oops! I could tell it was going to be Lecture Night at the Pikes'.

Well, all the squabbling aside, the show was a huge success. We gave them a standing ovation.

Afterwards the kids gathered around us, beaming. "Did you like it? Did you like it?"

"*GREAT!*" Kristy shouted in her best drill sergeant voice. "*EXCELLENT!*"

"Have you got any sweets left over?" Claudia asked with a big grin.

"It was so funny," Mary Anne said, blushing. "I . . . I almost cried."

Logan put his arm round her and said, "Aw, it's OK."

"Ooooooo!" Haley and Vanessa screamed.

The kids were in hysterics. We were in hysterics.

I only wish I had it on tape.

15th
CHAPTER

I learned something from the BSC Follies. It wasn't so horrible to be imitated in a show. It was kind of flattering, in a way. I'd have felt much worse if I'd been left out.

Even so, I couldn't stop thinking about You Know Who. Mr Trout.

On Saturday night I had a dream about him. He was standing on stage to receive some kind of award. He was smiling from ear to ear. Everybody was clapping. He had to take four or five bows. Mr Kingbridge and the two Dollies were behind him, looking on admiringly.

Then, just as he started to give an acceptance speech, the three grown-ups reached over and pulled off his toupee.

The crowd started laughing at him. And his bald head started to grow and grow, swelling like a balloon. He burst into tears and screamed, "*Jessssssiiiiii!*"

I woke up with a start.

The smell of coffee and scrambled eggs wafted up from the kitchen. Mama was humming a song.

I got dressed quickly and went downstairs.

Daddy and Mama were both preparing breakfast. I could hear Becca, Squirt and Aunt Cecelia in the family room.

"Hi, baby," Daddy said. "Just in time. Interested in scrambled eggs?"

"Yes, please," I replied.

I sat at the table. Daddy served me my breakfast, then he and Mama sat with me.

"So, what are you doing this morning?" Daddy asked.

"Nothing," I said.

Mama started talking about the BSC Follies, but the conversation soon fizzled out. Soon the three of us were just munching away silently.

Mama and Daddy exchanged a look.

"Penny for your thoughts," Mama said.

I sighed. I cut my scrambled eggs into tiny pieces.

"A dollar?" Daddy asked. "Inflation, huh?"

I couldn't help laughing. I hadn't planned on dragging my family into the Mr

Trout mess. I'd told them a *bit* about him, just that he was strange and wore a toupee, that's all. I suppose I'd been too embarrassed to admit what had happened in class.

But now I needed to talk to someone.

I took a deep breath. "Well, remember that sketch about the Klingon?" I began.

I told them everything—the pranks, the Balding, Mr Trout's reaction. They listened carefully.

"Poor man," Mama said when I'd finished. "You have some cruel classmates."

Daddy shrugged. "Sounds like he needs to get out of the teaching field."

"That was what Mr Kingbridge said," I remarked. "But I still feel so guilty about what I did in the show."

Mama and Daddy both looked surprised. "Jessi," Mama said. "He was just an oversensitive man. That's all. You didn't do anything to him that wasn't done to the other teachers."

"I *know*! Everyone always *says* that!" I blurted out. "But don't you understand? So what if it's not my fault? *I* still made him feel bad! *My* imitation made him leave town! I just wish I could, like, talk to him."

My eyes were watering again. Mama took my hand. "What would you say if you could talk to him?" she asked.

"Well . . . tell him I'm sorry, and I didn't mean to hurt his feelings. Ask him to come back to school. Say I was wrong. . ."

That did it. I buried my head in Mama's shoulder, sniffling away.

Mama rocked me reassuringly. I felt like such a baby—but it was exactly what I needed right then.

"Jessi, darling," Daddy said softly. "Does Mr Kingbridge know where to get hold of Mr Trout?"

"I think so," I replied.

"Then why don't you write to Mr Trout? Tell him all those things you've just told us. That way you'll get it off your chest."

I hadn't thought of that. It wasn't a bad idea. "OK," I said.

I went up to my room and began.

It wasn't easy.

How do you write to someone like Mr Trout—someone who never even said hello to you in the corridor?

I tried, *Please forgive me for being so cruel*, but that sounded too dramatic.

I tried, *I am writing to inform you that I did not intend to hurt your feelings*, but that was too formal.

I threw away at least ten sheets of paper. At last I just gave up. But I went back to it on Monday night, and every night that week.

By Thursday I had it. I read it aloud
seven times, made tons of little corrections,
then copied it out again.

It went like this:

Dear Mr. Trout,
    Hi. I'll bet you
didn't expect to hear
from me. I hope you
read this letter all
the way through.
    I just want to say
I'm sorry. Not that
I was involved in
the classroom pranks.
I wasn't (except for
the book dropping), and
I thought they were
mean. But when I
played you in the
Follies skit, I thought
it was different then
that. Just fun. I
did not mean to
hurt you. I guess I
thought it would
be all right, because
the other teachers did
not mind.

But I know everybody is not the same. I understand how it feels to be made fun of.

Please accept my apology. Would you consider returning to SMS? I hope so.

Yours truly,
Jessica Ramsey

I showed the letter to my parents. Daddy said he'd *run* back to the school if he got asked as nicely as that.

On Friday morning, I brought it to Mr Kingbridge. He seemed a little surprised, but he agreed to send it.

A week went by, and I didn't hear a thing.

To be honest, I didn't expect to. But I was happy I had written the letter. And I thought a lot about Mr Trout—and about what I had done.

Little by little, I began to see that Mr Kingbridge and Daddy were right. Mr Trout was too sensitive to be a teacher.

After a couple of weeks with Mr Bellafatto as a teacher, I understood something else. Mr Trout had brought a lot of his troubles on himself. He never shouted, never told us we were misbehaving. He *let* us get out of control. Mr Bellafatto respected himself, and that made us respect him.

So was I wrong to feel upset? Was it stupid to write Mr Trout a letter?

I knew that letter by heart. But the more I thought about it, the more I realized part of it was wrong. I *hadn't* thought the sketch "would be all right". I had known Mr Trout wouldn't like it. That bald cap had made me feel creepy the minute I saw it. Why did I go ahead? Because Sanjita and Randy and Mara and all the others wanted me to.

I wanted to fit in. I was worried about what they would think of me.

And those were the wrong reasons.

Mr Trout deserved that apology.

On Friday of that week, I came home to find a letter addressed to me in a tiny, neat handwriting I didn't recognize. I ripped it open, and this is what it said:

Dear Jessica,
   Thank you so much for your letter. It meant a lot to me.
   I'm sorry you feel so bad. You needn't. I always found you to be a thoughtful, attentive student.

I certainly appreciate your kind invitation to return. But you must understand I simply cannot.

I have applied to a graduate programme in advanced computer studies. I'd like to go into research someday. Wish me luck.

My very best to you in the developments of your many talents.

Sincerely,

Michael P. Trout